I0594113

Second Chance

HUSBAND

THE FIRST TIME SERIES

CARRIE ANN

NEW YORK TIMES BESTSELLING AUTHOR

RYAN

Second Chance Husband

The Falling for the Cassidy Brothers Series
Book 3

Carrie Ann Ryan

Second Chance Husband

The Falling for the Cassidy Brothers series concludes with an enemies to lovers romance that has been a long time coming. August and Paisley finally figure out what they've been missing.

The first time I got married, I watched the man I love walk away from me.

The second time around, I'm the one signing the dotted line first—this one a man who I realized I never loved.

Once burned, twice broken, I'm done looking for love.

Only my first ex-husband seems to be everywhere I turn—at my work, with my friends, and eventually...in my bed.

I didn't mean for it to happen.

Twice.

But I know if I don't protect my heart, there will be nothing left of me if he walks away again without telling me why he did so in the first place.

I don't know if I can trust this new version of ourselves or if it's merely the heat between us striking hot.

After all, second chances only exist in my dreams.

And there's no such thing as a second chance husband.

Second Chance Husband
The Falling for the Cassidy Brothers Series
By: Carrie Ann Ryan
© 2024 Carrie Ann Ryan

Praise for Carrie Ann Ryan

"Count on Carrie Ann Ryan for emotional, sexy, character driven stories that capture your heart!" – Carly Phillips, NY Times bestselling author

"Carrie Ann Ryan's romances are my newest addiction! The emotion in her books captures me from the very beginning. The hope and healing hold me close until the end. These love stories will simply sweep you away." ~ NYT Bestselling Author Deveny Perry

"Carrie Ann Ryan writes the perfect balance of sweet and heat ensuring every story feeds the soul." - Audrey Carlan, #1 New York Times Bestselling Author

"Carrie Ann Ryan never fails to draw readers in with passion, raw sensuality, and characters that pop off the page. Any book by Carrie Ann is an absolute treat." – New York Times Bestselling Author J. Kenner

"Carrie Ann Ryan knows how to pull your heartstrings and make your pulse pound! Her wonderful Redwood Pack series will draw you in and keep you reading long into the night. I can't wait to see what comes next with the new generation, the Talons. Keep them coming, Carrie Ann!" –Lara Adrian, New York Times bestselling author of CRAVE THE NIGHT

"With snarky humor, sizzling love scenes, and brilliant, imaginative worldbuilding, The Dante's Circle series reads as if Carrie Ann Ryan peeked at my personal wish list!" – NYT Bestselling Author, Larissa Ione

"Carrie Ann Ryan writes sexy shifters in a world full of passionate happily-ever-afters." – *New York Times* Bestselling Author Vivian Arend

"Carrie Ann's books are sexy with characters you can't help but love from page one. They are heat and heart blended to perfection." *New York Times* Bestselling Author Jayne Rylon

Carrie Ann Ryan's books are wickedly funny and deliciously hot, with plenty of twists to keep you guessing. They'll keep you up all night!" USA Today Bestselling Author Cari Quinn

"Once again, Carrie Ann Ryan knocks the Dante's Circle series out of the park. The queen of hot, sexy, enthralling paranormal romance, Carrie Ann is an author not to miss!" *New York Times* bestselling Author Marie Harte

To the one who said I couldn't.
I did.
To the one who said there was no chance.
There was.
And to the one who never saw me at all.
I'm here.
And so are they.

Chapter One

Paisley

"I now pronounce you husband and wife. You may kiss the bride."

It felt as if those words were an echo cascading within my own memories—as if there was no way those words had been spoken to me not once, but twice.

And both times, just a reverberation, a faded version of what I wanted. Or perhaps what I'd thought I'd been set on a path toward, with no ending in sight. No beginning, begging me for my attention and passions.

"With the power granted to me by the great state of Colorado, I now pronounce you..."

"Just sign here on the dotted line," another voice said, though they all blended into a similar vibrato. The real, the memory, the imaginary—all part of a whole.

Only I knew what voice *should* be the real one in this instant.

After all...it was my ending.

As an owner and financer of multiple businesses and someone with the power to change the destinies of others, at least in the business sense, I had signed my name on the dotted line countless times.

I knew every flourish, every flick of the pen, and every movement of my wrist as I signed. I was quick, efficient, and not verbose.

And yet, with this final signature, it would be an ending.

An ending before I was even ready for a beginning.

"Ms. Renee."

Renee. Oh yes, that was my name. At least part of it.

I looked up at the sound of the lawyer's voice as he frowned at me. "Is everything not to your liking?"

To my liking? That didn't make much sense, did it? Because that would mean I would have to like being here. But there was no way I wanted to be here in this moment, with these people, signing my name to a piece of paper that would once again prove I was a failure.

But, then again, my signature did more than that. I was powerful, I was competent, and I made my own way. That's what my signature evoked. It provided hope for others, it provided safety for me.

It proved I could handle anything.

So I would handle this. Just like I had the first time.

I gave my head a minimal shake. "No, we went over this a few times, the details have been ironed out."

Without looking at my lawyers or the two people across the large desk, I signed a promise. Or perhaps it should have been called a broken promise.

I wasn't signing my life over, wasn't giving it away; I was finding a way to make it my own again. And then I handed my lawyer the pen and scooted the divorce papers toward him. "Thank you, will there be anything else?"

There was a slight cough across the table, and I did what I hadn't wanted to do this entire time. I turned to see Jacob sitting there, a slight smirk on his face, even while anger burned in that gaze of his.

Jacob Barton, my newly ex-husband.

After nearly two years of marriage, we had proved to be a failure. Of course in his eyes, I was the only failure, and he was the one who had to deal with the inadequate wife.

For the Bartons of Denver, Colorado, were royalty— in the strictest of society sense. His grandfather had been a governor, his father a senator, and Jacob Barton would one day rise out of the ranks of lowly local politicians and become governor of Colorado himself. That was always in his dreams.

I had thought I had been the one in his dreams.

Instead I had kept my name, kept my business, and kept my path.

I hadn't become the wife he had wanted.

It was something I should have been used to as this wasn't my first marriage and divorce. In fact, I was becoming quite an expert at failing at relationships.

I still held on to one of the names I had kept in a divorce, because I was young and stupid and hadn't known any better at the time. I didn't know about or understand the paperwork of changing your name. The first time was atrocious, let alone doing it again. I'd gone through the entire process to wipe my first mistake from my life, and yet I'd kept it as a middle name—an albatross around my neck to remind me to never make that mistake again.

And that was the excuse I had given myself and Jacob when I hadn't taken his name.

Just another mark against me.

Never the perfect politician's wife. Just the ball-buster who couldn't even bother to love him enough to change for him.

I raised a single brow at the man I had thought I

loved but then realized I had made a mistake the moment I said, "I do."

"Are we done here?" I asked again, my voice chilly. I'd practiced the tone for years so I could blend in with the boys' crew of my job and place in life. And I knew with every word, with every brittle edge of my sentences, it would cement who I was in Jacob's eyes.

A frigid bitch not worth the paperwork.

And that was just fine with me.

"Yes, everything's done." He droned on about the legalities of what had just occurred, as if signature after signature hadn't cut ties between two people who should have never been together in the first place. "Each of you had prenups, and the paperwork splits everything evenly. Any shared assets are divided 50/50, but as you barely had any, this divorce was simpler than most."

Simple. I didn't scoff, neither did Jacob. But the rage in his eyes, that was anything but simple.

I hadn't told my best friends or anyone else that this was happening. The only person in my circle who knew I was divorcing Jacob, or in his words *he* was divorcing *me*, was my mother. Because there was no way I could ever hide anything from that woman.

I was more of a failure in her eyes than I was to Jacob, but I didn't have enough caffeine in my system to deal with those kind of mommy issues.

"Yes, all nice and tidy," Jacob said after a moment, but I wasn't sure what I was supposed to say back to him.

I had married this man because I thought I loved him. Or maybe it was because I had clung to something that wasn't quite mine. How was I supposed to know that falling for somebody because you were trying to run from another person and those feelings would blow up in your face?

And as spectacularly as they have now.

"Say hello to Lydia for me. Or don't. I don't care anymore."

His eyes tightened, and there was the anger I had learned to expect from him. He had never growled at me, yelled, or made me feel like I was nothing until our wedding night. And that was the first time, and *only* time, he had hit me.

He had said it'd been an accident, and I hadn't believed him, but he hadn't done it again in the nearly two years we had been married. Of course the past six months of those had been dealing with the divorce. Things would have been complicated beyond what they were now if we hadn't had the paperwork in place for the seemingly inevitable failure of our marriage. As he was of the Bartons of Colorado, which meant his family money outweighed most, having a clear and precise prenup had all been inevitable no matter who Jacob married.

No, it didn't outweigh my own business, but he was old money, in this case of Colorado old, and I was new money. The two simply weren't the same.

I was the trash who wouldn't take his last name, and wouldn't laugh at all of his jokes, and wouldn't spend my nights and weekends placating him.

I wouldn't lean into him as he called me worthless, as he gave me little digs to tell me I wasn't enough.

That man wasn't the Jacob Barton I had married. Or perhaps it had been the entire time and I just hadn't realized it until it was almost too late.

Or perhaps until it was too late.

I'd be forever grateful that I hadn't taken his last name. He had hated every minute of my independence from him and now it brought me a sort of joy.

After all, I still carried August's last name. Even my company carried August's name.

Talk about self-deprecation and turmoil. I surely loved hating myself more than any ex-husband could hate me.

Jacob's jaw tightened, but he didn't say anything. Of course Jacob Barton of the Colorado Bartons wouldn't. He would wait till behind closed doors then he'd tell you that you were worthless and you wouldn't be anywhere without him.

But that was Lydia's role now.

Lydia Sampson, the mistress, soon-to-be Lydia Barton. They would get married soon and quietly and everyone would whisper. But they would never whisper about Jacob.

No one whispered about him. No, because he was the golden child, and I was the whore. Which was funny considering I hadn't cheated.

Perhaps I hadn't loved him like I should, but how were you supposed to love when you had already had your heart shattered once before?

I stood up from the table and turned, my stilettos making sharp and echoing sounds down the marble hallway as I left the chambers of the high-end lawyers.

The divorce had cost far too much, but not in just money. My pride had taken a beating. And soon I would have to tell my best friends and coworkers I had failed. Because Devney and Addison were both married, happy, and mothers. They had the sweetest little babies, and the best lives.

And I was so freaking jealous it wasn't even funny.

Only it wasn't their fault they had married attentive and caring men. Who maybe growled a bit, but not as much as their brother. Because of course Devney and Addison had married brothers. The *Cassidy* brothers.

Heath and Luca were the cream of the crop, and I had appreciated them and cared about them. After all, they had once been my brothers-in-law. Because I was the one who loved making mistakes.

I had not married merely one man who had tried to break my heart; no, I had married another man who had succeeded at doing so.

August, Heath's twin, had been my *one true love*.

I rolled my eyes at my own ruminations, my ankles hurting from my damn heels.

No, not my one true love. You would have to believe in that crap in order for it to happen. So I didn't believe. Maybe for others, but not for me.

I was not the pretty princess who would find her prince. Nor was I the knight who would slay the dragon. I didn't have to believe in fairy tales. I just needed to get what was mine.

And that was not a man, not a happy ever after, and not anything to do with what I had once thought I wanted.

So I would make my business the best out there. I would make loads of money and give as much of it away as I possibly could to help other businesses. I would be the ice queen, no princess title for me.

I'd be the one that the other men at the board meetings and golf resorts would whisper about.

That ballbuster who didn't give a shit about men and maybe even ate them for breakfast.

That shield would be much easier to wear than any crap some silly thing like a divorce could hover over me like a mantel of whispers of what could have beens and my past. I wouldn't wear the title of Jacob's former flame and cover myself with the label also-ran as a shroud.

Jacob Barton of the Colorado Bartons would live on in infamy, and dust off this divorce like a silly mistake people would whisper about but never truly talk about. He would marry Lydia and have two point five kids and one day would become the governor of Colorado before a scandal broke out and he would either rise above it with his newly crowned wife at his side, or he would fade away into the distance and still make boatloads of money.

Because that's what happened to people like Jacob.

My phone buzzed in my purse, and while I looked down at the screen, I still ignored it.

My mother was not a happy camper. In her eyes, my biggest sin hadn't been marrying far too young and being left nearly at the altar for someone not good in enough in her eyes. No, it was how could I ever walk away from Jacob?

It didn't matter that Jacob had hit me once. Degraded me. It didn't matter that he had cheated on me and had never loved me. I couldn't walk away from that type of notoriety.

Too bad I was never good about pleasing my mother.

The only time I'd ever made my mother happy was when August, a high school chemistry teacher, and a man I thought loved me as much as I loved him, had walked away.

And I hadn't fought back.

Because in my mother's eyes why would I lower myself to fight for something that nobody wanted? And the only regret I ever had was that I hadn't fought. But what was the point? What was the point in pretending I had the strength to fight for someone who didn't want me?

I shook off those thoughts, ignoring my mother's call, and got into my Mercedes, pulled the top back, and drove like a bat out of hell toward my home.

The wind blew in my hair, the sun shined bright over the Rocky Mountains, and I laughed.

It was either laugh or cry and I had done enough crying.

Maybe I should call my friends; maybe I should tell them what had happened. But not tonight. Tonight I was going to be anyone else but me.

Because Paisley Cassidy Renee did not know how to live. She failed at everything that had to do with life.

So I would *not* be Paisley tonight.

I would be a stranger.

I pulled into my three-car garage, the door closing behind me. As soon as I got inside, I quickly changed into something far more comfortable. My shoes had pinched my feet, but I wanted to look like the part of the ice queen Jacob hated so much. I hadn't been the woman he had wanted, so I would be the woman that I needed to be.

A stranger for the evening.

I slid on too-tight jeans, the ones that hugged my ass in a way I knew meant they would probably tear if I bent too quickly. I slid my feet into cute boots with only a slight chunky heel. Then put on a top that tied at the breasts, and opened up so you could see some of my upper stomach, but it still flowed down over my hips slightly. I pulled my hair out of its bun and fluffed it into the soft waves that had come from leaving it up all day. I added a bit of eyeliner, gloss on my lips, and stuffed everything I needed into a tiny bag that I could wear on my wrist.

I looked like I had in college, just a bit older, a couple of lines at my mouth. They called them smile or frown lines, and in this moment, I didn't know where they had come from.

But it didn't matter.

Instead, I would just be someone else for the night.

I didn't look like the Paisley people knew. And that was fine with me, perfect in fact.

She didn't know what she was doing.

I called a rideshare and got into the back of a smoke-blue sedan and listened to odd techno music as the driver slung around the highway. He dropped me off in a nice part of downtown, but not the upper areas. One with a few restaurants, a bookstore, and a dance hall.

"Here you go," he said, popping his gum in his mouth.

I smiled, leaving an extra tip because he had gotten me here on time, even though the car smelled like weed. However, it was legal here, so I didn't care.

I got out of the car and made my way to the dance hall. Oh, I should probably have eaten something; probably should've been doing anything but this. But I had never been there and always wanted to.

It was a line dancing bar, complete with country music streaming through the speakers, and a live band would start at eight.

It was also apparently ladies' night, and two-dollar well drinks sounded right up my alley. I had become the champagne ice princess at one time, but now it didn't matter.

Now I was a different Paisley. One who was going to drink those two-dollar well drinks and be anyone else.

Because this Paisley, she wasn't working. Everything kept breaking, so I was just going to have fun.

I immediately did a shot with two random women who seemed to be on the same path as me. We nodded in agreement, as if no names were needed. Tonight was just going to be about dancing.

And so I got on the dance floor and moved to the beat.

I had decent rhythm, though I had no idea how to line dance. Thankfully people kept showing me how, laughing with me, rather than at me, as I tripped over my own two feet.

A couple of men got a little handsy, but I was the ice princess with my shroud of *back the fuck off* for a reason. And so they walked away, hands up with a single glare, and I kept moving within groups of women, feeling oddly safe, if not a little tipsy.

I needed to go home eventually, to cry it out, or just scream it out.

But first I was going to dance.

And just pretend.

Four drinks in, and I was not sloshed, but tired. So I

14

did another shot. And then another. Nothing mattered in the world, and the dancing just felt good.

I laughed and I smiled, and I felt like I had no worries. It didn't matter that I had to work the day after tomorrow. And I would probably be working tomorrow on the countless other things I had to do.

No, I was just going to be a new me for a few more drinks.

I chugged some water, made a friend in the women's restroom as she was crying over an ex, and I told her of course that he didn't matter, and she was going to find someone she loved eventually.

So I did another shot with her, and then went to dance with her friends before moving on to another group.

There was nothing like a women's bathroom at a club. You made the best friends there.

I kept dancing, ignoring my phone, and decided I would have one more drink and head home. See? I was being responsible.

Of course, the room kept spinning just a little bit even though I had quit spinning. So when I tripped over my feet, I wasn't surprised.

I expected the floor to reach me quickly, and I would probably bruise my ego as well as my body along the way. I wasn't expecting to fall into a hard chest, or to keep going until he was forced to catch me completely.

And I sure as hell wasn't expecting to look up into those familiar gray-blue eyes.

And there he was, my ex-husband.

No, not the one I had divorced today.

The one who had branded my soul, and my name.

August Cassidy looked down at me, eyes wide before they narrowed in anger.

Oh, I knew that look well.

It seemed I couldn't escape my past. Not even this new me.

Well, if hell was going to open up and take me, they might as well do that while I was in August's arms.

Because I still loved this damn man. At least part of me.

It might as well be him that I threw up on because I'd had too much to drink.

Reunions were always far too sweet for either of us.

Chapter Two

August

As Paisley fell into my arms, I had to wonder exactly how I had gotten there.

Then again, this seemed my lot in life. The one time I left my house to go on a date and enjoy myself, life literally fell into my hands. The memory I couldn't escape blinked up at me, wondering what the hell it had missed.

And of all the bars in Colorado, of all the honky-tonks I could have gone to, of course my ex-wife had to be in this one.

The sarcasm slid through me quickly, even as I wrapped my arms around Paisley's shoulders and side, keeping her close to me before she could hit her head on the floor.

I wasn't about to let her get a concussion because I let her fall to the ground.

Of course, at the time when I had been angry over the world and had seen her again for the first time after so many years of not wanting to, maybe I would have been a little slower to catch her.

No, that was a damn lie.

Because the only person that was going to hurt Paisley...was me. And that was only emotionally. I would never actually let anything touch her.

Including the goddamn floor.

"Paisley?" I asked, pulling her up so she stood in front of me, blinking slowly.

"Oh. It's you. That sounds about right. Of course it's *you*."

Dakota moved forward, placing her hand on my arm —her soft curves pressed against my side.

"Are you okay, miss? Let's get you some water. August? Can you keep hold of her? I'll go get her something to drink."

"You're really nice," Paisley said, her voice only slightly high-pitched. She wasn't even slurring. And if you didn't know her, you wouldn't realize that her words were coming out a little too quickly, a little too energetically.

Paisley Cassidy Renee was drunk off her ass.

I looked over her head, scanning the crowds to see if anyone was coming for her, but other than the few people who had given her a look of either concern or a roll of an eye that she had tripped and nearly fallen, nobody was even paying attention to our little tableau.

"Did you fucking come here alone?" I barked, and Paisley just lifted that chin of hers, a gesture I used to find sexy as hell, but now just saw the disdain and brokenness in it.

"I'm an adult, August."

Dakota looked between us, confused. "You two know each other?"

"She's a friend of my family's," I answered, not quite a lie.

Paisley just snorted, as Dakota smiled wanly. "I'm going to go get that water now."

I held back my sigh, aggravated over circumstances I couldn't change. "We have a couple bottles in the car. Let's just get her home."

Dakota stared at me for a moment, before nodding. "You're right. That would probably be smarter. And honestly, the line is getting long. You have your purse?" she asked the woman in my arms. Dakota was so freaking nice—which helped in her job and why we'd gotten along so well, but I knew she'd have questions for me about this little encounter I didn't want to answer.

Paisley nodded, before looking as if she regretted the action. "I do. Thank you. That is kind of you."

My date smiled wanly. "No problem at all. Come on, let's get you home."

"No, I was just going to call a car. You guys can enjoy your date. I shouldn't be out any longer."

My arms tightened around Paisley, before forcing myself to relax marginally. She was still swaying, so I didn't let her go completely, and thankfully Dakota didn't look as if she minded.

Oh, this was a great date with my current girlfriend. One where I was literally holding my ex-wife up before she fell on her face because she'd had too much to drink.

Where the hell was her husband?

I gritted my teeth at that thought, hating the fact that she even had a husband. Though I didn't know why it should bother me.

Paisley and I were exes for a reason. A reason I didn't want to think about.

"I'm okay. I'm just going to call someone."

"Let us help. We don't mind." Dakota smiled, before reaching to take Paisley's hand. "Think you can walk?"

"Yes. Sorry. I was doing fine, until I sort of spun a little too quickly. The ceiling isn't spinning anymore."

I reluctantly let go of Paisley as she held my girlfriend's hand, and the two of them walked toward the door.

"You're really pretty though. And nice."

Paisley was drunk. It wasn't that she wasn't complimentary. In fact, she was genuinely a nice person. She just wasn't so gushing usually, so outspoken socially like this. I didn't think I had ever seen Paisley this drunk, at least not since we had both been eighteen, and in college, drinking Smirnoff Ices behind the club.

That was a memory nobody needed to have on hand.

"You're very pretty as well. And I think you're nice too. Come on, August's SUV is over here."

"So you got rid of the truck?" Paisley asked, as Dakota gave me a look.

I sighed and followed the two women through the parking lot.

"A few months ago. It had over a hundred thousand miles on it and was getting too expensive to keep up. So this is my new pride and joy. An SUV. Look at me, an adult."

I had bought it new since used prices right now were astronomical, and it made more sense to just buy new, even with a loan.

I wasn't like Paisley who would probably snap her fingers and buy three Mercedes SUVs without even worrying about her bank account. Hell, even both of my brothers could probably buy a car without stressing as much. But I was a high school chemistry teacher. I didn't really know what not worrying about money felt like. I had student debt, a decently paying job, at least decently as far as being a teacher. And I was nothing like the millionaire businesswoman and tycoon in front of me.

No, I was much more like Dakota, the high school English teacher who made me laugh, made me smile, and made me think about things that I hadn't thought about in a while.

Dakota was safe.

Paisley was not.

And why the hell was I even thinking about comparing the two? It wasn't fair to either one of them. Dakota was nice. She always had a kind thing to say about someone, could recite song lyrics from every Top 100 song from her senior year in high school, and could outrace most people if there were coupons involved. She was also one of the most caring people I knew. Hell, she was helping a drunk woman I clearly had some connection to while we were supposed to have been on our date.

It was the one night a week where we didn't worry about grading papers or parent-teacher conferences or what the administration wanted us to do. Instead we would go out, dance, eat, and then come home and make love before going to our separate houses. Because we didn't live together and worked far too many hours, we couldn't spend too much time together, but it was something. It was steady.

My brothers and my sister each had marriages that worked and were starting families that thrived. They had lives that didn't revolve around me, and I was grateful for it. They had a steadiness that just made sense. And I didn't know if the kind of life they were living was exactly for me. After all I had been the first one of us to get married, and the first one of us to go down in flames. And I didn't want to be like my parents.

My parents were the epitome of selfishness. They had been married to each other not once, but twice. And they had gotten divorced the same number of times. Now they were together again, having dated each other this time for over two years. They had broken up a few times within those two years, but as far as I could tell, this was the longest they had been actively together without being married.

I had a feeling it had more to do with the grandkids than anything. They never cared about what they did to my siblings and me, they only cared about each other. Whether it was love, hate, or anything in-between.

After all, every time they had gotten divorced when we were kids, they had split the family up. And not in a way that made any sense.

No, they had decided to Parent Trap us. Dad had taken me and my brothers, and Mom had taken Greer, our sister. So for years at a time we didn't get to live with Greer. We barely got to see her, and visitation meant our parents got to see the other kid—or kids—but they rarely brought us along.

So when Greer had moved out to Colorado to start over with her best friend, falling in love with not one, but two men in the process, we Cassidy brothers had followed. We had watched her walk down the aisle and marry the two loves of her life, and we had been there for her.

Now all four siblings lived in Denver and had created a family and connection we hadn't been able to enjoy in our younger years because of how our parents acted in the past.

I pulled myself from the memory and looked on as Paisley and Dakota were talking to one another—Dakota being patient and Paisley doing her best to be the same despite the booze in her system.

"I'm really okay. I can just call a rideshare."

"No, August is going to take you home."

"He is nice like that. Sometimes." Paisley rolled her

eyes, and nearly fell again. I reached out and gripped her hips, keeping her steady. But the moment I touched her, something familiar washed over me, and I set her straight again before dropping my hands.

"You're swaying, I'm not letting you get in some stranger's car."

"You don't get to tell me what to do."

"Yes, because you're making so many good decisions right now."

"August, why don't you take care of her, and I will head home. You've got this. And I don't want her to be embarrassed by having a stranger watch over her."

I turned to Dakota, confused. "What do you mean? You're going to leave me with her?" Why did I sound so panicked right then?

"Take her home. I'll see you tomorrow. Okay? We can grade papers together." She went to her tiptoes and kissed me softly, her hands on my chest.

I kissed her back, oddly confused what was going on, before she pulled away and waved, and got into her car which she had parked next to mine. We were supposed to be dancing right now, before heading to her house, enjoying the night, and then I would head home. It's what we did.

But of course, my poor decision changed everything.

"She's truly pleasant," Paisley said, before sighing and resting her head on my passenger-side window.

With a groan, I got Paisley in the car and buckled her in. She looked slightly green, and I certainly hoped the hell she didn't vomit in my new car. I closed the car door, and she pressed her head to the glass, snoring through the window.

What the hell had gotten into her? Why weren't my sisters-in-law with her? Because of course my ex-wife would become best friends with the two women my brothers had married. Hell, she even hung out with Greer, even though they also had a past since everything having to do with my family seemed to be complicated. Nothing made any sense anymore, and I was way too confused right then.

I got into my seat, turned the car around, and realized that I had no idea where my ex-wife lived. I could investigate her little purse on her wrist, and hope for the best, but hell, I wasn't in the mood to figure it out.

"I guess you're coming home with me," I grumbled, and pulled out of the parking lot.

Paisley slept the entire way, snoring loudly—something she only did when she was sick or stuffy headed. The only times I had seen her drunk in the past, I had been equally as such so I hadn't noticed before.

Hell, something was wrong. I probably should call

Addison or Devney, my sisters-in-law. They might know. They could probably handle this for me. If I had been a smart man, I would've just dropped her off at one of my brothers' houses and washed my hands of it. But no, they were probably doing the things that new dads did, and spending time with their families. They had lives, lives that didn't need to involve me, or me literally foisting my problems onto them.

With a sigh, I made my way to my house, took the Herculean effort of getting Paisley out of the SUV, still woozy, and got her inside. When she made a hiccupping sound, I cursed and picked her up, cradling her to my chest, before dashing to the nearest bathroom.

I set her down in front of the toilet as she emptied her stomach.

Cursing, I pulled her hair back from her face, not liking how clammy she felt.

She heaved mostly liquid into the basin, and I let go of her only for enough time for me to get a washcloth and soak it with cold water. When I pressed it to her forehead, then the back of her neck, she let out a groan that was a little too familiar.

"Thank you," she whispered.

"You're welcome," I grumbled.

This wasn't exactly how I thought I'd be spending my date night—helping my sick ex-wife empty the contents of her stomach. Contents that seemed to be just alcohol.

"Did you not eat?" I snapped.

"I meant to. I just wanted to forget."

Forget what?

But I didn't ask. I didn't want to know.

I didn't want to know anything else about Paisley. Because if I did, every single regret would come back, and I didn't have it in me to breathe through those anymore.

When she got sick again, I took care of her, and when it seemed like she was finally done, I used another washcloth to wash her face, and then I carried her to the guest room.

With a sigh, I stripped her out of her clothes, not because of anything nefarious, but because I knew she wouldn't want to sleep in them, no matter how tight those jeans were. And she probably felt as disgusting as I felt just then.

She helped me pull on one of my old shirts over her head, and a pair of old shorts that barely stayed tight around her waist. She drunkenly stumbled into bed, and I tucked her in, pushing her hair back from her face again.

"I'm going to get you some water, and some ibuprofen. Okay?"

"I'm sorry."

I frowned, pulling back. "What for?"

She licked her dry lips, her eyes filling with tears before she did the most Paisley thing ever and blinked away any sense of sadness. "I'm sorry for ruining your night."

I shook my head, annoyed with myself. "It seems like you wanted to do that on your own first. At least to yourself."

She pressed her lips together, and I was afraid I had been too mean just then, but I didn't know what else to say. Instead she blinked again and swallowed hard. "I just wanted to be somebody else. Just this once."

That didn't make any sense to me. Paisley was remarkable. Despite the fact that we fought all the time, she was a powerhouse. And I loved watching her soar. She was brilliant, amazing, and *married*.

"Why, Paise?"

She was silent for so long I thought she had fallen asleep, but then she opened her eyes, and I sighed. "Why do you want to be someone else?"

"Because nobody wants to stay when I'm me. Maybe they'll stay if I'm someone else."

And then she closed her eyes, and promptly fell asleep, her words daggers right in my fucking heart.

Chapter Three

Paisley

The tap-dancing gorillas that were currently working on a special piece for the morning did not want to let up anytime soon. The fact that they were on my temples at the moment, practicing with their little tap-taps and oddly delicate sashays, meant that if I opened my eyes, I might actually die. That could be the end of life as I knew it.

Of course, because I had the memory of an elephant, I could remember exactly what had happened the night prior, and why I was currently having an imaginary conversation with those tap-dancing gorillas from my headache.

I knew I must have been near the end of my sanity as I was apparently leaning into the circus and safari themes of my nightmares. Or would they be daymares now because I could sense the sun cutting through the blinds that were not my own as they shone over my closed eyelids.

Of course. Of course.

I was ridiculous in so many ways, but never in ways that I let others see. In fact I was usually good about keeping my ridiculousness at bay.

It wouldn't be great for the world to see Paisley Cassidy Renee act as if she did not know what she was doing. She couldn't be the ridiculous one without any sense of knowledge or kindness.

No, she had to be steady.

But I hadn't been her last night. No, I had been the insane one who had decided to drink far too much. And not only had it been so unsafe, but I was lucky I hadn't made even more mistakes than I already had; it was also just another reason that led me into my current hell.

I took a deep breath, pushing all memories and thoughts I did not want to focus on out of my mind so I could do the unthinkable.

I opened my eyes.

With a deep breath, I then promptly shut those lids. *No. Too much sun. Way too much sun.*

The tap-dancing gorillas had now been joined with a trio of violin-wielding crocodiles who had decided to serenade me with their hell.

Was I still drunk? That was quite a possibility. One never knew these days.

Especially when it felt as if I was never going to be able to recover from what had just happened.

And it wasn't even the current pain residing in my skull, or the fact that as I opened my eyes one more time, the light blinded. No it was none of those things.

It was because I knew *exactly* where I was.

I wasn't at home. I wasn't in a stranger's bedroom after a night of intoxicating sex in which it was all mistakes and terrible decisions. No, it couldn't be a stranger. I couldn't have even been kidnapped by a crazy knife-wielding man. No.

I had been saved by my ex-husband. No, not the one that I had divorced yesterday. But the one that had divorced me years before.

And there were always going to be those qualifications, weren't they?

Because Jacob and I had divorced each other, even though he had cheated on me, we had divorced each other. Much to my mother's painstaking disappointment.

But August? He had left me.

And now here I was, sleeping in what had to be his guest bedroom, and under his roof for the first time.

Why was it that it couldn't only be embarrassment

crawling over my skin? No. It had to be something worse. Was that pity for myself—no, it couldn't be that. Was it pain? That made a little more sense. Because I didn't know why I would be feeling like this. I *shouldn't* feel this way.

With some distinct effort, I forced myself into a sitting position and took stock of my situation. I had no idea where August was. I didn't even know if he was in the house. Maybe he had left me here and gone to his girlfriend's home. I held back an audible groan at that thought.

His girlfriend.

I had no room to talk. I had been married until late yesterday afternoon. I should've been happy he had moved on. With a nice, caring woman who hadn't even blinked about the fact that the man she had currently been dating had left with a drunk woman in the passenger seat. Or maybe the woman was completely clueless and maybe August did that often. Helped drunk women and stuffed them in his guest rooms.

It had taken me a moment to realize *why* I had been in his guest room and not my home. Because of course August didn't know where I lived. I didn't know where he lived either. In fact I had no idea where I was. I had no idea if we lived in similar neighborhoods, or on opposite ends of Denver. Because Denver wasn't just main city Denver. If you said you were from Denver, you could be from one of over a dozen suburbs. We all lived in different towns within Denver. Whether it was Arvada or Littleton or Westminster or Centennial. All of these places still counted, at least when you talked about the grand scheme of things. In fact, I had driven through two suburbs to go from the lawyer's office to my house and then back to the bar. So for all I knew, I could be neighbors with him or be an hour away.

Then again, I had been countless miles from him even when I thought he had loved me. So what did I know? But no, I had things to do. I would schedule a car to get me home—after I found my clothes, because I was currently wearing shorts and a shirt that were not mine. I was at least wearing my balconette bra and panties, so there was that. But he had seen enough. Of course his mouth had been over every inch of me at one point in our lives, and while I didn't look exactly the same, I shouldn't be too embarrassed. I had probably thrown up all over my clothing, and he was just trying to deal with the smell. I was a disgusting mess.

And of course, even through my drunken haze, and that hangover that would not quit, I could remember exactly what I had told him the night prior. I could still hear the words seeping through my lips as I sat on these blue cotton sheets with the stone-gray curtains not blocking out the sun.

This place looked homey, with a few odds and ends I remembered from our shared home. As if he had tossed things in this place that didn't have a certain space for it in the other parts of his home.

I needed to get up and get through this. Live through the embarrassment, and my own disappointment, and then get home.

And then I could get through the rest of my day, and my life, and be the complete disappointment that I was to everyone else. It was what I was getting good at.

I slid out of bed, grateful I didn't fall flat on my face. After I took one wobbly step, I put my palms in front of me, rolled my shoulders back, and let out a breath.

"You are Paisley Fucking Renee. You can do this."

I didn't dare mention the Cassidy part of my name when I was in a home of a Cassidy. It was like summoning Beetlejuice or something.

At least that's what I was telling myself.

I quickly went to the restroom, took care of business, and was grateful when I saw a toothbrush there, with a little sticky note with my name on it.

Ever the organized teacher, he had thought of everything.

And I hated the fact that I still missed the sight of

his handwriting. What the hell had I drunk last night? Memories and regrets?

I was never doing that again. Even if I had to search for the Paisley I wanted to be for the rest of my life, the drunk dumbass one was not going to be it.

At least that righteous anger at myself could push away some of the disappointment and utter agony seeping through my system. *Was it seeping?* No, it was a tearing, an utter grating as it ripped through my organs, reminding me that they would scar me until the day I let out a breath that was the end of my nights.

I couldn't find my clothes, but hopefully I would find them once I got out of this room. I pulled my hair back in a ponytail with the elastic on my wrist, washed my face, and I figured that was all the dignity I could muster.

It wasn't like I could find anything else.

I rolled my shoulders back, opened the door, and stepped into the hallway.

The scent of bacon sizzling filled my nose, and the sound of the news filtering through the air hit my system.

August was here. And this was his home.

Not our home.

I let out a breath, and walked with my chin held

high to the kitchen of the man I thought I had been in love with.

August stood there, his back to the TV as he worked on breakfast over the stovetop. He had on an olive-green Henley, with the sleeves pushed up to his elbows, and worn jeans that had seen better days. He had bare feet, and his hair pushed back from his face. It was a little longer than I was used to seeing him with, and it curled a bit at the nape of his neck.

With that rugged jaw of his and the slight beard he wore, he was a beautiful man. Rugged, but with a great smile that honestly reached his eyes.

I hadn't seen that smile aimed at me in a long time.

He did smile though, he showed emotions when it came to his nieces. He was the sweetest man with his family. And I was grateful he had that.

Because I wasn't sure I would have ever fit in that way with his family. After all, I had barely seen them during our short disastrous marriage. We had been young, in love, and apparently stupid.

"Your coffee's on the counter. If you're done staring at me."

I blinked, and swallowed hard, wondering how long I had been standing there, and when he had noticed.

"I also set down some water, and another ibuprofen if you want it. Breakfast is almost done."

Again he wouldn't look at me.

Damn it. Why was I here?

But that coffee looked good and smelled even better. I took three steps toward it, and looked down at the mug, at the perfect coloring of that coffee. With just a dash of cream, and the sweet scent of chicory.

"Thank you," I whispered.

Because he had made me coffee exactly how I liked it in the mornings. I could go for lattes or espressos or any other type of coffee later on. Even cold brews if I was feeling it. But my first cup of coffee in the morning was chicory with a little cream. And he had remembered.

I took a sip, and the taste exploded over my tongue, nearly sending me into bliss as my eyes pricked with tears.

I hated him so much just then. Because he had left.

Like they all did.

I set my mug down and reached for the water before taking the two pills.

"Do you want to tell me what happened?" he asked as he turned to me, a plate in hand. He set down the bacon and eggs in front of me, and my stomach roiled.

I shook my head and immediately regretted it. I was hungover, and I only wanted this coffee.

"Eat. It'll help your stomach."

"I'm fine. Thank you. The coffee's good."

He just grunted.

And then he stared at me, and I knew if I did not at least take a bite, he would continue to glare at me until the end of our days. Because the only friends I had in this town I loved happened to be related to this man. So I was never going to be out of his vicinity until the end of my days. Because that was my lot in life.

With a sigh, I took the fork he had set down next to the plate and cracked the yolk on the over-easy egg. My stomach rumbled even as nausea waved over me, but then I set the fork down and dipped my bacon into the egg.

August's jaw tightened at the look of it, but I ignored him, letting the saltiness spread over my tongue so I could breathe.

I continued to eat, and after a few more bites, he dug into his plate, eating in methodical bites without looking at me. The greasy food along with the piece of toast he had buttered to perfection next to the eggs seemed to settle my stomach, even as I tried not to break down.

"You need to tell me, Paise."

"I'm fine."

And I hated when he called me Paise. I would never call him Augie, as I didn't like the name, and the only people who called him Augie liked to be jerks to him. But he had always called me Paise when he had smiled at me and joked around. And I hated it. Because I was not his anymore.

"I'll tell the girls. I'll call them right now and they'll get it out of you."

I looked up from my empty plate, surprised I had finished, and narrowed my gaze at him. "Fine. I got a divorce yesterday. And I wanted to celebrate."

I hadn't meant to blurt it out, but the news would hit the cycle soon, as the Barton family was infamous in this town, and my business dealings led to some media attention. But I had wanted to tell the girls first.

Instead I was telling my first ex-husband that I now had a second. I was so winning at life.

August just blinked at me. "What the fuck did Jacob do?"

And why did it feel like he had hugged me in that moment, emotion running its sharp prick of anxiety and hope into my heart at the fact that he thought it was Jacob.

That Jacob had hurt me.

No, Jacob couldn't hurt the iciness in my chest. I had frozen over long ago and I hadn't even realized the full extent of it until I had been able to so easily walk away from Jacob, the man who had cheated on me.

No, the person that had broken me was standing right there in front of me.

Just like the other person who had completed that shattered mess looked at me every time I stared into a mirror.

We were one and the same, my reflection and his past, and I never wanted to drown in that memory again.

"It just didn't work out," I said icily.

"Did he hurt you?" he asked, his voice so low it was barely above a whisper.

My spine straightened, and I shook my head, this time not feeling nauseous. The breakfast and meds with coffee had worked.

Damn the man.

"Not in the way you think."

Except that once.

I didn't say it out loud.

August's eyes narrowed anyway. "I'm going to kill him," he growled.

Despite that odd sensation that slid through me at the words, I immediately raised my chin. "No. You will not. It's done and over. And I'm sorry for putting you out last night. Please apologize to your date as well. Thank you for helping me not make another mistake."

"Paisley..." he began.

I held up my hand, before sliding my dishes into the

sink. "No. I appreciate all you've done. But I am going to go get dressed, and then call a car. I will do dishes after I get dressed, so don't worry about it."

"I can do the fucking dishes."

I didn't flinch at his tone. "Fine. Then thank you again. For everything. Please tell your date that I'm sorry."

"Dakota wasn't upset. But I'll tell her you said that. Do you want to talk about it?"

"Not in the slightest, August."

When he froze for that instant, I realized I did not say his name often. How odd to think that between us that he was the one who said my name, and I tried never to say his. What did that say about me?

"What are you going to do about the vacation up in the mountains we're all going to soon?"

I cursed under my breath, as I had forgotten the damn Cassidy vacation. I hadn't even wanted to go, and Jacob certainly hadn't. It was probably because he had been so adamant about not going, that I had gone full head into helping the girls plan the damn thing.

August's two brothers and his sister, as well as all of their spouses and children were going to be at this event. It was a lovely vacation in the mountains for the families, and the girls had wanted me to come, because I had become part of their family, though not August's. When August had said he would be fine with it, as he was going to bring a date, I thought why not. So I would bring my husband, and we'd all be one happy family in this modern world.

And now I was in a new hell. This time with mountain peaks and skiing.

"I'll cancel, or I'll go. I don't know. You don't need to worry about it."

I would just be the seventh wheel. But you know, I was used to that.

"You don't need to get a car. You don't need to cancel. Let me just drive you home."

I took a step back from him, needing that armor again. "If you'll just point to me where my clothes are, I'll do that."

"Your pants are over there and your shirt is in the washer. I have one of Greer's shirts for you though," he said, speaking of his sister.

For some reason I was grateful that it was his sister's, and not his girlfriend's. But I wasn't going to lean too hard into those thoughts. That way lay so much trouble.

"Thank you. I'll get it back to you." I sounded so prim and polite. I hated myself in that moment.

"Paisley. I'm here, you know. If you need me."

I just looked at him then, wondering exactly when this had occurred. And who this man was.

"I'm fine, August. I will be. Thank you."

And I quickly called for that car service and got undressed. By the time I was ready, my little purse and phone in hand, the dishes were done, the news was off, and August was in his office. Probably grading papers or doing the countless other things he did as a teacher. He worked so many hours, probably just as many as me, but never got a thank you.

I wanted to say something, but I wasn't sure what there was to say. Instead I left a note, something simple, just a goodbye and a thank you.

And then I walked to the car, grateful my driver didn't say a word. I could have hired my actual car service, instead of a rideshare, but I hadn't wanted to deal with the questions from my staff. So instead, I made my way home, to the place that was not Jacob's, but just mine, and locked the door behind me.

I should have expected the slap.

But then again, life came at you fast when you weren't paying attention.

Pain ricocheted over my face as I staggered back into the door and looked into the eyes that were so like my own.

"How could you," my mother spat, and I lowered my head, letting out a breath, knowing she wouldn't hit me again. But I could deal with her yelling.

I always did.

Chapter Four

August

"But why do they call it elephant toothpaste?" Kyler, my most inquisitive student asked, and I just smiled at him, loving this part of the lecture.

"That much you're going to have to see."

"I saw this on YouTube," Brayleigh said from the back, and I put my finger above my lips though I didn't touch them since I was still wearing gloves. "Let's not spoil the surprise, shall we?"

"I promise I won't. It's fun." She gave me a conspiratorial smile, and I nodded, then I looked over at my class.

"Okay, today we are going to talk about catalyst reactions and surface tension. Are you guys excited?"

Some of them cheered, others just looked bored.

That was about par for the course when it came to high school chemistry.

I taught chemistry, as well as life sciences, and AP courses. I also did some extra tutoring on the side, as well as textbook manipulation and codes. Meaning I did a lot of fucking work for little pay, but I didn't mind it.

Today we were going to have a little fun in the lab, rather than sitting in a course where they would look as if they had no idea what I was talking about, even though we had already read the material. Some people would go on to enjoy this in college and learn new things, others would just laugh it off, and promptly forget it ever happened.

However, if I could make a few kids laugh, and enjoy learning science for just an instant? That was worth it. That moment when they finally connected and understood what was going on around them? That was it.

I had already worked with the hydrogen peroxide, and the food coloring inside had swirled to an intriguing purple color that matched our school colors. I could have put drops along the inside of the rim of the bottle's mouth so that way the foam in the end would create stripes, but I decided to go with this.

I added the dish soap, and then on the side, mixed yeast and warm water while explaining all about the reaction in front of me. Some people took notes, as it was going to be on the quiz the next day, and others looked bored.

However, when I poured the yeast mixture into the bottle, I stepped back, enjoying the reaction.

And not just from the chemistry in the bottle.

A large foamy mixture poured out of the bottle, continuing to pile up on the counter, with increasing force.

People gasped and cheered, while some scooted back in their chairs. This was a perfectly safe reaction, one I had done countless times, and I freaking reveled in it.

"So, let's talk about what makes this foam appear," I said with a laugh.

"So that's why it's elephant toothpaste? Because it's big enough to brush an elephant's tooth?"

"Perhaps," I said with a grin, as we went into discussing hydrogen peroxide versus yeast as they broke down into water and oxygen. "Since oxygen is a gas, it wants to escape the liquid. But the dish soap that we added to the reaction traps those gas bubbles, forming a foam. And now you're going to watch me clean this up because the janitors at the end of the day don't like it."

They laughed as we segued discussing how hydrogen peroxide turns into just oxygen and water.

"So that's why hydrogen peroxide comes in the dark bottles? To keep it fresher longer?" Brayleigh asked, seemingly interested even though she had already watched this on YouTube.

I smiled brightly, loving the fact that she got it. That glow in her eyes? That's what I wanted from my students. Yes, I wanted them to have a good time, and to learn, but the need to learn more? That desire to enrich your brain? That was why I was a teacher.

I had only gotten my master's degree in chemistry and I hadn't gone on for my PhD. While I had known that schools would have been able to give me stipends and pay for my degree because larger schools wanted those contracts from the government and other platforms, I hadn't been able to take the time. I had needed to start my life, and frankly, working for industry, or even at a college level had never suited me.

I liked working for high school.

I liked the long hours and dealing with teenage angst. Because I liked providing the steppingstone for kids to realize that there was something beyond wanting to be what their parents thought they needed to be.

Yes, my course was required for the school, and they would also have to take the college equivalent if they wanted to be a doctor or a pharmacist or anything with a shiny label, but there were countless other things that they could do. And even if they didn't go into chemistry or the sciences, maybe it could spark their creativity for the arts or something else.

That's why STEM was no longer STEM, but STEAM. Because you needed the arts in order to appreciate and enhance the science behind the knowledge. And as I explained that to my students, a few rolled their eyes, but others smiled.

These were my junior levels, who would possibly take AP chemistry next year, and that also meant they were working on deciding their majors already, as well as looking at colleges, and taking their required tests.

It always surprised me that we as a society decided a fifteen-year-old or maybe even younger was the right age to decide what you wanted to be when you grew up. I had made that decision early because I enjoyed it.

But then again, I had thought I'd wanted to be an astronaut as well.

I hadn't realized I wanted to be a teacher at this level until college, but I had wanted sciences. Just like Heath had gone into business, and I was pretty sure he hadn't realized he wanted to own bars like he had in Oregon and now Colorado. Luca was a vet, and a damn child prodigy at the end. He had finished college before I had and was already in vet school by the time I was deciding what I wanted to do, even though he was younger.

But it didn't bother me. I wasn't jealous of him or how quickly he'd finished school. Luca had gone through his own aches and pains along the way, and so had I.

Of course, Heath had been through the worst of it. I ran my hand over my heart as I finished cleaning up at my desk and collected the papers I would need to grade all night so I could stay on top of things.

Heath was my twin. We were identical in looks, and sometimes in nature. I was mostly the growly asshole unless I was at work. Because being a growly asshole chemistry teacher meant that my kids weren't going to like what they were doing. And it was a hard enough subject for some that me being that asshole would just hinder their progress.

So I had to fake it to make it.

But Heath? He was affable. He had always been that way, even when he had been a little kid, sick with the cancer rotting his body. My twin, the person I had literally shared a womb with had been sick, and I hadn't been.

I had been perfectly fine, and I had watched my brother dwindle down to almost nothing, until he had gotten better.

And now he was far stronger than I was, with a lot more muscle, and a bigger beard. The guy just oozed health and vitality and was a great dad and husband to boot.

And I felt like the brother left behind, wondering why the hell I thought it would be a good idea to move out with all of them, and end up being next to my ex-wife.

I pinched the bridge of my nose as I made my way to the parking lot, annoyed with myself.

There was literally no reason for me to be wallowing in my own self-doubt and pity.

It had been years since I thought about my brother being sick, and the fact that I hadn't, even though we had had the same genes. Such a weird thing to think, considering I had enough going on.

Like the fact that my ex-wife had slept at my house, and I hadn't heard from her since.

How the hell was she divorced again?

Yes, she could be icy at times, a little brittle around the edges, but she had her reasons. I knew I was one of them, but I wasn't going to fess up to that in the moment. However, I had never liked Jacob.

That asshole had consistently looked down on us. He'd only come to two functions at the Cassidys', and while that made sense considering it was his wife's ex-husband's family, it was also his wife's friendship circle.

But apparently, we Cassidys had never been enough for him.

Of course, the one time he had sneered down at my sister, let's just say he was lucky he hadn't walked away with a bloody nose.

It was only Paisley giving me a long look about my anger that had stopped me.

Because I knew Jacob had been a judgmental asshole about the fact that my sister had two husbands. She was in a committed relationship with two men who also loved each other, and it was a poly relationship that worked.

However, Jacob hadn't seen that. But me punching out Jacob's lights for protecting my sister would not have gone well with the rest of the family. Because then they would have thought I was just some jealous asshole when it came to Paisley.

And that couldn't be further from the truth. I was not jealous when it came to her. She was just an acquaintance. Not even a friend. Because being a friend would mean that I would have to care about her more than I did.

And I didn't.

Not even in the slightest.

I made my way to my SUV and looked up to see my

girlfriend leaned against the back of it, looking down at her phone.

Dakota was beautiful. Dark chestnut hair she had pulled back into a soft braid for work. She had on those linen slacks things that billowed around her ankles, and a top with some form of crocheted books on it. She looked sweet, nice.

And way too fucking good for me.

She was just a good person. And I knew that I might one day fall in love with her, but I would never have that burning passion that had broken me before. And that was what I needed. Something calm, something nice.

Something trusting.

And someone who understood the fact that being a high school teacher was a lot of fucking work, but worth it.

She looked up at the sound of my approach and slid her phone into her bag.

"Hey," she said, and there was something in the sound of her voice that worried me.

Her gaze searched mine, and I frowned at her, reaching forward to brush her hair back from her face, a single strand that had fallen from her braid. She didn't lean into the touch like she usually did, instead she just studied my face, beseeching.

"How was your workday?" I asked, delaying what

felt like the inevitable. That should have warned me something had changed beyond this moment, but instead I stood there. Waiting.

"It was long. I'm testing today. I have papers to grade. So I guess I'll make this short."

Dread curled in my stomach, but not in the way that it should.

I didn't love Dakota. But I liked her. We were still new at this. Maybe I *could* love her. I had only loved one person in my life, and I didn't know how that had happened. How I had fallen. A part of me had been finally ready to maybe figure it out. Or at least be better at pretending.

"That was her, right?"

I blinked, confused at the question. "What?" In the next instant though, I realized who she had to be talking about. The only woman I'd been near Dakota with. The woman I'd driven away with even if it had been Dakota's idea.

Dakota swallowed hard, and I watched as her throat worked. "The woman that broke your heart. That was Paisley the other night at the club." She let out a soft sigh, her gaze suddenly so serious I felt the ache in my bones. "You never told me her name. But I saw your face."

I shook my head, annoyed that I had been so transparent. "I don't know what you're talking about," I lied. "We don't have time for this. We have to get through that assessment coming up." I was pulling at strings, and no one was left to pick up the threads. I wouldn't have blamed her for pushing me away physically at this point.

Dakota shook her head. "No, you never have time." She let out her breath, but I didn't say anything. I wasn't sure there was anything to say at all. "I can see I was fighting an uphill battle from the start."

I frowned at that, honestly confused. "What are you talking about? What does she have to do with any of this? What does she have to do with *us*? I'd told you I'd been married before. But that was in the past. She's just a family friend, Dakota."

"She is the person you should talk to. And by the way, mentioning you were married but still apparently hanging out with your ex-wife without being clear means you either don't have respect for her or you have none for me."

"Whoa." My eyes widened, honestly shocked. "I never meant for her to be a problem." I winced. "Okay, poor choice of words. What I meant was if you were ever in a setting where she would have been there, I would have prepared you. But she's not my ex-wife in those circumstances. She's my sisters-in-law's friend. They met her outside of whatever past I might have had with her. I didn't even know she lived here until I found out she was Devney's boss."

And wasn't that a shock.

"It's hard to believe you right now, August."

I held back a curse. "I promise it's the truth. She's not...I'm not...she's in my past, Dakota."

I reached for her, but she stepped back. "No. I think we're done. Because I know you're not going to be the right guy for me. Not when I can see that I'm clearly not the right person for you. And that's okay. This was nice. We both said we were going to make this casual, so it didn't interfere with work. So it's fine. But I saw the way that you looked at her. And even if that never works out, I can't be second best. You deserve more than that, and so do I. So we're going to be friends like we said. And I'm just going to leave now."

"Dakota..." I began. However, I wasn't sure what I was supposed to say. She was right. I didn't love her. I thought maybe I could try, but the only reason we had started dating as coworkers was because we had been friends first, and I figured when it all went to hell, because it inevitably did, as it did now, we would be able to remain friends.

But I didn't see hurt in her eyes, just resignation.

As if she had been expecting this.

Maybe I hadn't been as good about hiding my asshole self as I had thought.

She turned on her heel then and left, walking back to her car. It was still daylight out, though the sun was setting, but I watched her drive away, making sure she was safe. That was the least I could do.

Thankfully there was nobody else heading to their cars right now, nobody to witness that, so I got into my car and headed home, a sigh escaping me.

I pulled into my garage and brought my bag inside, knowing I needed to work.

I had finally moved on, and my fucking ex had ruined it again. Maybe that wasn't fair to Paisley. Maybe it was my own fault. Or maybe I just needed to get better about being over the first woman that I had loved.

The only woman that I had loved.

What kind of complete asshole was I?

I set my things on the counter, then went to the dryer, remembering I hadn't taken care of the laundry that morning since I had been running late.

I pulled out the thankfully dry sheets and went to the guest room. The guest room where Paisley had slept, leaving her scent all over the sheets. I had immediately stripped the bed once she had left, not needing her scent to remain there, but I was notoriously terrible at finishing the laundry, so it had taken me two cycles to get them clean. And now I made the bed, erasing her completely from this house. Too bad I couldn't erase her from my life. Because she would always be there.

I didn't know how she was going to handle dealing with the fallout of that divorce, or what my family thought about it because the girls had to know by now. The divorce would be public anyway, because her ex was that big of a deal, at least in these circles, but I shouldn't care.

I should care about the fact that Dakota had just dumped me because she had seen my expression when I had looked at Paisley. Though I didn't even know what that expression was. I didn't love Paisley anymore. We hadn't worked out, the divorce was long over, and she had been married and divorced since. I just hadn't wanted her to get physically hurt. Not out alone and drunk. Because it was a stupid choice on her part, but it would have been selfish of me to have left her on her own in the state she was in.

But then I wasn't sure what I was supposed to say or do in the moment.

Because Dakota had seen it, even though I hadn't.

And now I was dealing with those consequences.

I finished making the bed, and then pulled out a beer, figuring I could just heat up leftovers for dinner. I sat down at my desk, sipped at my beer, and looked at my bag filled with papers I needed to grade.

I had work to do, a life to live, and I would apparently be doing it alone.

Which was better than the alternative. I'd been pretending to live a life that made sense. As if I could walk through life in my orderly way and not grow attachments to anything real. Again, pretending. And I had gotten far too good at it recently.

However, a small part of me reminded myself this was exactly what I had asked for. What I had wanted.

I had been the one to leave after all.

So I didn't have a leg to stand on, even if it created my own situation, and I ended up being alone surrounded by others.

At least it was something I was good at. I had plenty of practice, after all.

Chapter Five

Paisley

Thankfully the headache from hell had only lasted a day. But now I had a brand-new headache.

One that might have something to do with my mother, but I was better off when I pushed that to the side and focused on my job, and not the fact my own mother hated me.

There were enough people out there with mother issues, I didn't need to publicize mine.

As I signed the paper in front of me, I let out a breath at the familiar feeling. Because once again I was signing papers, but at least this didn't have anything to do with my divorce.

At least I didn't think so.

Two of my associates sat in front of me, each of them

having worked hard through the ranks in order to be where they were. They were brilliant, hardworking, and were the best at what they did. I hired the best, and I also hired those who could get there but needed a little help. Because not everybody had the ability to pay for a four-year school or take time off when needed for certain jobs. I had single mothers, adults who were raising their younger siblings, I had widows who were getting full-time jobs for the first time in their lives because they had been stay-at-home moms. I had people who were changing careers and trying to find their path. I also had others who couldn't afford retirement yet thanks to corporate greed, or the way that the world was working. I took everyone in that I could and found them a place to help us all survive in this world and thrive.

Only I didn't feel like I was thriving right now.

No, I felt like the two people in front of me weren't staring at my signatures, but rather the bruise I had tried to cover up.

They couldn't see the bruise of course. It was only a slight one, that was mostly a red mark. I had been clever with concealer and bronzer, and they wouldn't be able to tell that my mother had hit me. After all, I should have been expecting that slap from her.

They may not have been able to see the bruise, but I could feel it. My mother rarely hit me. She hadn't as a child, just a quick few slaps here and there when she wasn't getting her way.

And while I realized as an adult that was never okay, I knew others had it worse. After all, I had been able to get out.

I just hadn't realized my mother had found a way to get my house key. Something I would be working to change soon. New locks. New keys. New security.

Because damn that woman and everything she represented.

My mother had paced in front of me while I'd done my best to stay steady. "How could you? You were supposed to stay married to him. We were going to be someone. We had power. And you threw it all away because what, he didn't like your cold vagina and heart?"

I had scoffed at her, walking away. Of course, my mother would go straight to sex and feelings as if she had a single drop of care for another person who could penetrate her reptilian skin. All she had wanted was for me to be the perfect little pawn in her grand schemes. It was odd though because I had never realized my mother had such grand schemes. Before, it had been beauty pageants when I had been little, making sure I was the prom queen, and any little part of our small town into the big city where I could shine under her glow. Or maybe it was the reverse? I wasn't quite sure where that metaphor had taken me, other than the fact I couldn't escape this woman.

I had tried to escape to Colorado. But apparently, I hadn't gone far east enough of Oregon. My business was settled here, and we were thriving in this atmosphere. Even if I had to deal with the Bartons, even if I had to deal with my mother, we were kicking ass and taking names. Even if today's signature didn't quite feel like it.

I wasn't going to change my life and uproot everything to run away from my mother. I'd done it once before out of sheer desperation and grief, and in the end, I'd only been able to because of the circumstances shrouding me. Moving on and starting over had just been an advantageous consequence of the interactions set forth by those around me and those I'd willingly made. Although she had ended up following me anyway.

No, I had run away from my problems and memories, and they had still come to bite me in the ass.

This time the wrong decisions suffocating me didn't push me onto a dance floor...no, I wasn't going to go down that memory lane—not with how I'd ended up that night.

"Is everything okay, Paisley?" the woman in front of me asked, and I nodded tightly, not letting her see beneath my shell. There were only two people who worked in this building that truly saw who I was, and sometimes I was afraid even they didn't see that.

Devney and Addison were off today, as our company only worked four days a week—at least most of us did. I tended to work seven days a week, but I didn't examine that too closely. However, with those two out of the office, the people who could truly see what I was feeling and knew too much weren't here. So I had a little bit of time to keep hiding the bruises that had nothing to do with the one on my face.

"I'm sorry, my mind's going a mile a minute working on other things. But this paperwork looks fine."

"That's true, but it doesn't have to be final if you don't want it to be," Jessa said softly, and I gave her a strange look. "You were the one who helped push for this sale. After all, we didn't build the company, it was an acquisition we helped strengthen, and now the former owners want to move to a different company, settled in Europe and not here."

"And you don't have to do that," Dawn whispered.

I stared at the two of them, frowning. "What's going on? This is a matchmaking company, one that is doing well, unsettled, but we don't need to have any stake in it. We did what we wanted to accomplish. We helped build it up. Now we're going to sell it. Just like the former owners who will still have a stake in the business want. Talk to me."

Dawn swallowed hard. "We were just thinking. You know. About the optics."

I raised a single brow. "And by optics, what do you mean?" I ask, though I had a feeling I knew exactly where they were going with this.

Jessa cleared her throat. "Well, it might be prudent to put off selling a matchmaking firm until news of your divorce is no longer on the press's mind."

I tilted my head as I stared at them, trying to hold back any sign of emotion.

Of course now that the divorce was public, people would be talking about it. Since I first walked into the building, people had either given me pitying looks, or darted their gazes away.

I shouldn't have been surprised people didn't know how to act around me now. No one truly understood how to as it was. I'd been their boss, their savior, their ice queen, and now the topic of their gossip.

And while I was used to people not understanding the labels they etched into my skin whether well-intentioned or not, I wasn't in the mood to deal with the outcome of the divorce today.

I didn't want their pity, their knowing looks. I didn't want the questions in their gazes.

Was I good enough for the Bartons? Why had we divorced so quietly? And quickly? Was I at fault? Of course I was. It couldn't be dear Jacob because he was perfect. Perfect and pristine just like his golden boy image would always be.

And when he got married to dear Lydia, everybody would continue to see him in his golden image with sparkles and unicorns coming out of his ass. They wouldn't see him for who he truly was.

They would see me for who they thought I was.

The cold bitch who couldn't keep him.

Now I apparently needed to get rid of this match-making service.

Not that there was anything wrong with that business. However, two days after my divorce wasn't the time to speak of it.

"I'm not quite sure why my relationships have anything to do with the matchmaking one. It wasn't as if I met my ex-husband through this service. They're not going to connect the two. I don't know what you are worried about."

Though I did. We all did.

Dawn shook her head. "Maybe we should wait on it. I'm sure the owner will understand."

"I think we should continue on as we have. Leaning into what the media wants to flame isn't going to help.

After all, if we move on as we always have, they will ignore me. I'm not worth talking about. Our business is. So let's keep on track, shall we?"

They both nodded, and though I knew I sounded harsh, I didn't want to talk about this.

We had things to do. And dealing with what the media thought was appropriate wasn't it.

I sighed, wondering exactly how my life had gotten to this point. Although I guess it was my own fault. I had made the poor decision to marry the man. And while selling a matchmaking company while a divorce was being settled probably wasn't the smartest idea, there wasn't anything I could do in that moment. We just had to buck up and move on.

At least that's what I kept telling myself about it.

At least nobody told me to try out the matchmaking company. Of course, if I continued down this path, they would probably mention it. So I pushed for the next agenda item and kept moving on.

My phone buzzed more than once, and while some messages were from my mother, others were from my friends.

The news had broken, and I hadn't been the one to tell them.

That was possibly childish of me, or just cowardly. But I wasn't quite sure what else I was supposed to say.

I didn't want to tell them I was a failure.

By the time I found myself alone, knowing that I needed to meet the lawyers to finish signing the paperwork for the matchmaking company, my phone was ringing off the hook. I would have to call Devney and Addison back, but they weren't the only two getting through. My two administrative assistants were fielding as many calls as they could, but they couldn't catch them all.

It seemed the media had truly caught wind of the divorce, and the firestorm was just settling in.

I ignored my calls and went to my emails, knowing that I couldn't ignore those.

Everybody wanted a statement on the divorce, wanted to know the whys of it, wanted details. It was none of their damn business. However, I knew I wouldn't be able to just leave it to Jacob.

I quickly called out for my publicist. "Clark—"

He didn't even need me to finish my sentence. "I'm on it. We have the three statements that we prepared just in case. Do we want to go full tilt, vague, or down the middle."

I already saw the headlines, as it seemed Jacob's team was taking a firm stance. "We'll go down the middle for now. No mention of cheating, or even the phrase of irreparable differences. We just move on. Like we need to."

"You've got it." He paused for a minute, and I let out a breath.

"What is it, Clark?"

"Are you okay? I know you don't usually let me ask. But you don't have to do this alone, you know. Jacob's an asshole. We need to make sure that the world knows."

"It's not my place to tell the world he's an asshole. They'll see it soon enough."

He snorted. "He's a politician, honey. People are going to vote for him because he's an asshole."

That made my lips twitch. "So me telling the world that he cheated on me isn't going to help. They're going to be able to figure out the timeline soon, connect the dots. I won't be the scorned woman in their eyes. There's no need for me to ice down the narrative where I sound like a jealous bitch."

"That is true. But you know that I'm in your corner, right? You've got people."

His statement made me smile. "I do. Thank you."

He cleared his throat again.

I held back a sigh. Clark was a fierce publicist who cared for his clients, but I didn't want him to look too closely. "What is it?"

"Talk to your friends. Addison already called me.

I'm pretty sure she's probably going to storm your office soon."

I pinched the bridge of my nose, that familiar guilt clawing its way through my gut. "Thank you for letting me know."

"You're welcome. Now, we'll handle this part, you handle everything else."

"It's what I do," I say with a sigh.

I looked at the clock then and realized it was after six. My team was already heading out, as I didn't force people to work for too many hours a day. And I knew if I left now, some might think I was leaving to lick my wounds, but I didn't care in that moment. I was tired, and I had more work to do at home. Plus, I had people I needed to reach out to. They were worrying about me, and I had to fix this.

Somehow.

I picked up my phone and looked at the group chat.

A dozen messages, and I knew I needed to answer them. To face the consequences of my own decisions.

Me: *I'm headed home. If you're able, I would love to see you there, with wine, cheese, and I'll tell you everything.*

Addison texted back first. I hadn't known her as long as Devney, but she was already one of my favorite people in the world.

Addison: *Damn straight. We were already planning on attacking you at home.*

Devney: *She means cornering you and asking questions, not actually attacking.*

Addison: *Well, I said what I said.*

My lips twitched.

Me: *See you in an hour?*

Addison: *You've got it.*

Devney: *I have sparkling wine.*

Me: *Sounds good.*

I sighed, continued to pack up, and then headed out. I nodded at a few people who were still at their desks, since I wasn't the last one out like usual, but then again, since marrying Jacob, I hadn't always been here for late nights. We had had dinner parties and media relations to deal with. Something I hadn't quite realized how much of myself I had given up until I stepped back to look objectively. And it had never been enough for him.

I wanted to shake my head and push him out of my thoughts, but we were going to talk about him tonight, so I wouldn't be able to do it fully yet.

But then I would ignore him, and everything that had come with him.

I would just be me.

Whoever that me was.

I made my way to my house, having put on an audiobook rather than listening to the news. Because at the first mention of Jacob's name, I knew that this wasn't going to let up anytime soon.

Our local world, and in some aspects the national one, wanted to know why Jacob and I had gotten a divorce. And our statements, not so joint at all, weren't going to clear the air. Because even if Jacob was going to throw me under the bus and it all be a lie, the affair would come out. Especially when his marriage to Lydia happened so quickly. But that wouldn't be on me.

And if I kept telling myself that, I would soon believe it.

I pulled into my garage, grateful I didn't sense my mother about. I had already changed the alarm key codes, and I would be changing the locks soon. I hated the fact that she had figured out how to worm her way in. Just like she always did.

I took off my shoes and stretched my ankles a bit after a long day in high heels. I went through my normal routine.

At least the normal routine that had happened since the divorce. I was trying to find it again since moving out of the mansion with Jacob, and into the home that I hadn't ever sold. I hadn't even realized that I had had a backup plan, a safety net, until I had needed it.

I slid into comfy lounge pants, a tank top, and a soft

zip-up hoodie, put my hair in a clip, and went to set out a few snacks for the girls. I had music playing this time, still not watching the news, as I had already read the headline news, as well as multiple news sources that had nothing to do with my life with Jacob.

There was at least that.

Then I went to start cleaning a bit, knowing that the girls would be here any minute.

However, when I went to the guest bedroom in search of a storage box, I saw one that made my heart ache.

Without thinking, and yet knowing it was a mistake, I went to my tiptoes and pulled down the memory box I had forgotten I had stashed here.

I sat cross-legged on the floor, the hat box on my lap, as I gently took off the circular lid.

It was odd to think I wasn't mourning a recent divorce. Oh, I might be mourning the person that I had been when I thought I'd been in love, but that had just been a mirage.

No, apparently now it was all I could do but mourn a relationship long gone.

I let out a shaky breath, annoyed at myself for even falling down this rabbit hole.

Inside were countless photographs, notes, movie tickets, and even a concert stub or two.

Mementos of a time long gone, of a lifetime that didn't even seem my own.

There was the time we had gone to a city park and shared a Frito pie, all the while laughing with the children as they giggled, playing within the park itself. I still had the receipt for that Frito pie, with a little smudge of chili at the edge.

The remnants had long since dried, and was probably disgusting, but I kept it. As well as the movie ticket stub from our first date.

There was the receipt for my wedding dress, a simple plain white dress I had found at a discount store. So unlike the extravagant lace and corset bodice I had been forced to wear for Jacob's mother as well as my own.

A single dried flower from my bouquet.

And scattered amongst the relics of a past better left forgotten, were photos.

Polaroids, printed out photos, and those little ones that you get from carnivals and arcades where they print out in a long strip.

We had been so young—August and me.

So young, and perhaps carefree, though not in reality.

We'd both been running from pasts when we hadn't even realized it. But I saw the love there. The aching love in both of our eyes.

When had that gone away?

When had August stopped loving me?

I could see now that Jacob had never loved me. As I looked back, I realized that my business and my connections to this new age of power in his eyes were why he had married me. I kept having to ask myself why I had married him.

But I never had to ask myself why I had married August. Yes, maybe I was clinging to wanting to have something steady in a world that didn't feel steady at all. But I had married August because I loved him.

And I could see the love in his eyes.

When had it turned to heartbreak? When had it turned to indifference.

When the doorbell rang, I quickly tossed everything back in the box, having jumped and watched its scattered remains hit the carpeted floor. Swallowing hard, I made sure nothing was out of place as I set the box down, and then wiped my face.

They would think I was crying over the asshole, or maybe the media attention. And that would be fine.

They couldn't know I was still in love with their brother-in-law.

They couldn't know how everything hurt.

I opened the door, and my two best friends stood

there, not a lick of pity on their faces, just caring because they loved me.

"So, do I get to cut off his dick?" Addison asked without preamble.

"That just sounds like so much work, and very messy," Devney put in. "I say we take a trash can outside and burn memories of him."

I just grinned at them, tears forgotten at the sight of the women who lifted me up rather than tore me down like the rest of the world seemed to try to do.

"I'd say we burn things, but there's not an inch of him in this house. No memories. No photos. Gone like that." I snap my fingers. "But you know what's not gone? That bottle of wine. Let's work on that."

"I love you," Addison said, she wrapped her arms around me hugging me tight. And then Devney was there, holding me too, but I didn't cry. I'd already done that.

And I had done so for a man they didn't realize I was mourning.

I wondered what kind of friend that made me?

I wondered what kind of woman couldn't let go.

But in the end, it didn't matter. Because I had all I needed. Friends, wine, and a box full of memories I wouldn't open again.

Chapter Six

August

"So you got Addison to take not only Keelie, but Hayleigh with her on a girls' night?" Greer asked as she sat down on the couch next to Luca.

"Yes, though I'm sure Devney will head on over to hang out with the girls once she's finished with her project." Luca looked over at Heath, who nodded.

"Yes, she doesn't usually work late at the office, but they were dealing with a firm in Tokyo, and needed to switch their hours a bit. I don't mind though, because it meant she was able to spend the last couple of days at the house, and rest." Heath rolled his eyes. "I swear, getting our wives to rest and relax these days is ridiculous."

I sat back and listened to my siblings discuss their

married lives, and who was watching the kids for the night. I didn't always feel left out of the conversation, as I was the only one not currently married, and unlike Heath and Luca, I wasn't a dad. However, for some reason, there was an odd sense of loss sliding through me. As if I was the one behind.

It wasn't as if I had thought I'd be married with kids by now; I hadn't put much thought into it. But I had been married once before. The first one to do so, even young and blind, and the luck that I had forsaken in the end. And now here I was, the single guy, though I wasn't quite sure that the others knew that distinguishing remark yet.

But I was the single one, the one who went home to an empty house.

It shouldn't have bothered me. I had a hundred other things to do during the day, and worrying about being alone didn't need to be one of them.

We were having a Cassidy sibling dinner, something we didn't have often. Mostly because our family had grown. Greer rarely had time to hang out with us brothers these days, though she had been the main reason we had all moved out to Colorado in the first place.

After our parents' marriages and subsequent divorces, it had been hard for us to figure out how to form a relationship with Greer. We brothers had always had each other through the turmoil of connections and lifetimes. But Greer had been alone. It didn't matter that we had tried to reach out to her. Our parents had cut off those lines of communication. I didn't know if they realized how painful and damaging those acts had been at the time. To them, they had been merely cutting themselves off from the other parent in the situation. But because they had gone all *Parent Trap*, they had lost out on getting to know their own children.

My father did not know Greer. Hell, I didn't know my dad these days either, but my father did not raise Greer. Just like Mom hadn't raised us boys. It never made any sense to me why they had done that, or why they hadn't allowed true visitation, but there was no healing those wounds completely. There was still a scab over the wound, one that every once in a while, our parents came back to pick.

However, when we had become adults and realized that we could make our own choices, we had done the unthinkable to our parents. We had moved to be with Greer and start the next chapter together as a family. I still wasn't quite sure what Greer had thought when she had looked up one day and seen her three hulking and overprotective brothers. It hadn't helped that she had been dealing with a monumental terror in her life at the time. Thankfully, she had had not one but two men in her life to lean on. Now she was married to both, living a life I hadn't expected for her, but also knew that it was perfect for her. Both Ford and Noah loved their wife beyond all reason. And I knew that they would protect her soul, as well as her, herself, and her heart along the way.

It was almost as if we brothers were superfluous when it came to her life, but then again, here she was, taking the time to hang out with us like we had wanted when we had first moved here all those years ago.

"Why are you frowning?" Greer asked, as she leaned across the table to tap my knee. She sat on the couch next to Heath, while Luca and I each had our own chairs on either side of them.

I shook my head at my little sister, glaring at her. "I'm not doing anything."

"Exactly. You're not part of the conversation. What's going on with you?"

"Thank you for asking, because he never answers me," Luca said with a roll of his eyes.

He leaned forward and popped a cube of cheddar cheese into his mouth, moaning at the sensation.

We had never been a true cheeseboard and appetizer family, but for some reason, Greer's husbands were, and suddenly here we were, having a cheese plate instead of a steak and baked potato and bagged salad like we had used to.

Of course, that probably was something stereotypical I didn't want to lean into, but as the sole single guy of our family, I felt like I needed to hold on to those traditions.

"You guys are just way too nosy," I said with a sigh, then froze at the sound of a yip.

Luca cursed under his breath and quickly scrambled up, heading toward the large bin in the corner.

"Okay, Sandy, you're fine. You just woke up from your nap."

He immediately pulled out the small cocker spaniel, as it woke up fully, licking at Luca's chin. The dog had a cast on its back foot, and looked pathetically tired, as if no matter how much sleep it got it wasn't enough.

Well, that sounded about right.

As we were at Heath's house, not Luca's, it should have been a little surprising that Luca would bring one of his work pets home, but of course that wasn't the case.

Luca continually had some form of foster animal with him, or one that needed to be watched throughout the night, or at least not be lonely and he didn't want to leave at his office underneath the care of some of his team.

"Sandy?" I asked.

Luca sat on the couch, Sandy and her cast on his lap, looking a little stressed.

"That's what her owners named her. We had to reset a broken leg, and then she had a couple of test issues I wanted to keep apprised of. She should be going home to her parents tomorrow, but I wanted to keep an eye on her tonight. And we're full up at the office with the rest of the staff. I didn't want Sandy to get forgotten because she's usually so quiet."

In fact, other than that one yip, I hadn't heard another peep from that dog. Which was odd because usually they barked in love and made little panting sounds when they were in Luca's arms.

"Is she going to be okay?" Greer asked, concern stamped on her face.

Luca nodded, running his hands down Sandy's back. She finally began to calm, resting her head on her little paws.

The dog was damn cute. At one point I thought maybe I would get a dog of my own, or even a cat. Luca had a whole nursery at his house, with animals coming in and out daily, as well as animals of his own he and Addison raised alongside their daughter.

At that moment, Luca's phone buzzed, and he cursed under his breath, looking down at the screen. "It's the office, I need to take this." Sandy looked up, worry in her gaze, and Luca sighed before standing up and moving forward.

Without even knowing what was happening, suddenly I had a sad cocker spaniel in my lap, whose eyes gave Luca a look of such betrayal for leaving her, that I knew my face probably echoed the same look.

"Pet her, before she shakes right off your lap," Greer said, and I looked down at the little dog who stared back up at me, confusion in her gaze.

I didn't know why those eyes of hers reminded me of Paisley's just then. Probably because I was losing my damn mind. But here I was, holding a dog and gently petting her. Maybe it was because Paisley had looked that sad before. As if she had been left behind.

Of course, those were the words she had said before, and I was supposed to act as if I knew what I was doing.

With a sigh, Sandy rested her head on her paws again, and finally relaxed, but I didn't stop petting her. If I did, she could get sad again, and I didn't want that.

Again, the correlations between her and Paisley worried me, but I didn't focus on that. I couldn't.

"You should get a dog."

I looked up at Greer, frowning. "What?"

"You should get a dog. Or a pet. That way you're not alone."

I raised a brow as she cringed. "Thanks for that assessment."

"Well, Greer's right," Heath said with a shrug, and I scoffed at my twin.

"I'm not alone." I blinked. "I have papers." The laughter following my statement wasn't as bright as I'd have liked.

"What about Dakota? Things getting serious there?" Greer asked.

I knew I should just calm down and not get annoyed that they were prying. But this was sibling time. When we all pried into each other's lives and then updated one another.

I slid my hands over Sandy's fur and sighed. I knew I probably should have mentioned it in the group chat, but getting dumped by your girlfriend while at work, all the while not realizing that you were calling her your girlfriend, wasn't fun.

"Oh. I'm sorry," Greer said as she leaned over the edge of the couch to pet my knee. Sandy took that as invitation and butted her little head against Greer's palm. My sister smiled, and petted Sandy softly, before Sandy rolled back into my chest, nuzzling into me.

Well, at least the dog liked me.

"It's okay. Dakota wasn't right for me. It's fine."

"She dumped you?" Heath asked, and as I glared at

him, he winced. "Sorry. I wasn't being a dick. I was just surprised. You guys seemed to like each other."

I frowned, not knowing why he would think that, since he had only met her a few times, and that was while we were at his bar having a drink. It wasn't as if I had invited her over for family dinners or anything. Maybe that had been part of the problem. That I hadn't invited her over for things. But we hadn't been there. At least I didn't think so. It was nice to have somebody, but I hadn't thought we were truly serious.

And as evidenced by her walking away, she thought the same. We weren't each other's forever. And that was just something the world had to get used to. I was sadly already over it. Which probably said something more about me than it did anything else.

Luca came out at that moment, and smiled softly at Sandy on my lap, but didn't move to take her. I didn't mind, as the dog was now snoring on me.

"So what'd I miss?"

"Dakota and August broke up."

"I'm sorry about that. She seemed nice." Luca was silent for a moment, and I just let him be until he asked the question he wanted to. "So, how is this whole vacation going to go with the family, with you not bringing Dakota, and I assume Paisley isn't going to bring that asshole Jacob."

I winced, as my siblings all grumbled something about Jacob. It was nice that we all hated the man, even though none of us had known him.

Although Paisley wasn't family, she had been around with the girls enough that it felt like that for them. Not for me, never for me. But the idea that none of us knew Jacob even though she'd been married to the man? That was all red flags.

And I hadn't caught it because I had been too busy trying not to be jealous over my ex-wife.

Not that it had worked well.

"We'll make do. We always do. It's not like we're sharing a room." I glared at my sister. "No setups. We're divorced. We're finally getting along somewhat. Don't screw it up."

Greer held up both hands. "I promise I'll be good. I'm just excited for the Cassidy family vacation. I know we could all use a break."

I nodded, grateful that my scheduled break within my school year lined up with the break we were having as a family.

It would be nice to go to a resort up in the mountains and just hang out, hike a bit, dip in the heated pool, and just be. I would probably end up bringing some form of curriculum to work on, but it wouldn't be too bad. Everyone else would be off with their families, kids and all, and I would be alone, with a drink, and the view. And far away from Paisley.

"I'm just sorry it happened before the trip." He cringed. "Well, that sounded selfish of me, but it's the truth. Bringing her to a family event like that was a big deal, and now...well..."

I shook my head at my brother. "It's fine. We still work together, and she isn't glaring at me. It just didn't work out. No hard feelings."

Again, that was a testament to something I did not want to think about.

"It'll be good for Paisley to get out of the city for a bit too."

I frowned at Greer's words. "What do you mean?"

"Haven't you been watching the news at all? Every single local gossip column is talking about it, and even the main local news mentioned it. The Bartons are big money here, and his sudden and secret divorce is a thing."

Hell. I hadn't seen it.

Because I had been avoiding it.

"Getting Paisley some time to breathe will be good, and I'm glad she's coming." Heath looked at me. "As long as you're okay with it."

I scowled again. "She's friends with your wives and Greer. I long ago gave up the idea that I could control how you guys dealt with her. It's water under the bridge. We're all adults."

They gave me a dubious look, but there wasn't anything else for me to say in that moment.

We continued to eat, and set Sandy back in her bin, comfortable in her memory foam padding.

"Seriously, this is the best cheese dip ever." Greer set her hand on her stomach and sighed happily. "I don't know when I started to love cheese, but I blame my husbands."

"Well, thankfully I'm not allergic to dairy, so I'm counting that as a win," Luca said with a sigh, and I understood since Luca was allergic to more than a few things.

We went to start to clean up when the doorbell rang, and Heath frowned.

"Who the hell could that be? Devney should be home soon."

"But she wouldn't be ringing the doorbell," I said, a little uneasy.

I followed Heath to the front door, as Greer and Luca went to check on Sandy. For some reason, I was surprised when I saw who was on the other side of the door, even though I shouldn't have been. After all, our parents had this odd way of knowing when we were happy and finding our way.

"Darlings," Mom said as she moved forward. I stepped back before she could hug me, her overly perfumed scent already filling the spacious room.

"I didn't realize you two were in town," Heath said, and my dad just smiled as if he didn't have a care in the world.

"You know we're in town more often than not, we love seeing our grandkids."

That was the truth. They did love their grandkids. I hadn't realized that parents could treat grandkids so much differently than how they had treated their own kids. I had thought that was just something you saw in movies. But whatever slight connections that both Heath and Luca gave our parents to their grandkids, our parents relished. They were decent grandparents. Although I knew that they never had sole visitation. No, there was consistently one of us nearby. Not that we thought that they would kidnap them or anything, but it was more the fact that we were used to their neglect. And their constant bickering back and forth. But the way that they were looking at each other, they didn't look as if they were fighting now.

"What are you guys doing here?" Heath asked, and I was grateful that we hadn't taken out any of the planning brochures and notebooks we had for the upcoming vacation. Our parents were not invited. They would make the whole thing about them and the trip would become far too difficult. There was no way that we were going to allow them to harm this time that we had for each other. The fact that they routinely seemed to know when the four of us were together alone though, it was like they had some form of psychic connection. Or maybe I needed another beer.

"We're here to tell you the good news. I know you have a thousand things to do, we'll leave soon, but we have news," Mom said, practically bouncing on her toes.

Greer and Luca came forward, the four of us standing in line against our parents.

I hated the fact that imagery was so close to the truth. It had taken far too long for the four of us to find each other the way that we needed, and yet, I knew no matter what happened, I would never let our parents hurt my siblings. My siblings each had families to take care of, so I would be the one that took care of them.

"What's the news?" I asked, my voice a blade.

My mom looked hurt at my tone, while my dad just looked annoyed. However, they both brushed those expressions off their faces before moving back to their point.

"We're getting married." Mom smiled up at me, showing off her brand-new engagement ring.

I frowned at them, utterly confused.

"I thought you two were already married?" I blurted.

"No, we were going to get married a couple of years ago, and then with your weddings, and the babies, we took our time. And then we had a little break," Mom said, as she looked over at my dad. I didn't even want to see what expression she had on her face.

Either she was reminiscing about the fight or relishing in it. I didn't want to know what side of the coin she had chosen today.

"Married? Again?" Greer asked, just as aghast as I was.

They had been married twice before, divorced twice as well. I thought they were already married, but apparently, they hadn't gotten to the deed before backing out again.

I had no idea how many times they had been together versus not in my life, and I didn't tend to dwell on it.

"Yes. Again. I love your father, and it's time for us to be a family."

Mom beamed as if she had said something profound, and instead dread just filled my gut.

These were the examples of love and forever in our lives. Two people who either loved each other without pause, while ignoring the rest of the world, or people who hated each other to the point that they had to tear down everything in between them, including their own family.

There was never a middle ground for them.

They kept changing their minds, falling in and out of love as if it were a trend.

And all I could think about was the fact that I had been the first to get married, the first to get a divorce, and part of me still loved the woman whose life I was no longer a part of.

Apparently, the apple didn't fall far from the tree.

And didn't that make for a lovely realization?

Chapter Seven

August

Honestly, I should have found a way to fake a cold. A broken leg. *Maybe I could actually break my leg.* Yes, all of that sounded a lot more reasonable than going on vacation with my two brothers and sister, two nieces, all the spouses, and my ex-wife.

Yes, I couldn't forget the fact that I was about to go on vacation with my ex-wife.

There had to be some form of medal for acting like a dumbass.

I knew there was probably a way to get out of this. However, disappointing my nieces wasn't going to be an option.

"Uncle August," Keelie whispered, and I leaned forward, grateful that she could now enunciate August.

I had been Uncle Agag for way too long. Hayleigh was right behind her with her words, and I was so damn grateful to be an uncle. "Can you sit by me?" she asked, her voice soft, her eyes wide.

I reached out and tugged on her tiny pigtail.

"I'm in the other car, with all of the things."

Seriously, every single thing we could possibly need for the house. Since I was driving up alone, they had filled my car to the brim with every single food item, game, or anything else that we could possibly use. We had booked a few rooms in a resort up outside of Vail, and though we weren't going to be skiing, we were going to be enjoying ourselves just as a family. But that meant entertaining each other, and two kids. "So you're not going to be with me?" she asked, her little eyes filling with tears.

It was like a kick to the gut to see my little niece hurting. But I also knew she was probably playing me. Maybe not on purpose, but she and her cousin both knew that if they asked me for anything, I would move heaven and earth to give it to them. It was just going to be a little more difficult for the next couple of hours while we drove up the mountain.

"I am going to hang out with you for the entire next week. You've got me. But you're going to be driving with your mom and dad up into the mountains."

"And I'm okay at driving right, baby girl?" Luca asked as he came forward, resting his chin on my shoulder. I knew he was making odd faces for his daughter, and I did my best to look stern, as Keelie giggled.

"Excuse me, I was having a conversation with my niece. Get out of the way, Daddy."

"I love you, Daddy. And Uncle August."

And right then and there, my heart just burst.

These kids were seriously too cute for their own good. I might not ever get a chance to be a dad, but I was a damn good Uncle August.

"Hey, August, you have a minute?" Heath asked, and I leaned forward to kiss Keelie on the cheek, before leaving her alone with Luca. We were at Heath's house, all of us packing up the cars for the fifteenth time. Devney and Paisley had the spreadsheet, and I was fine with them going through it all. Honestly, it just made sense for them to be the ones organizing this, because I was pretty sure if we were going into battle, I would want all three women, as well as my sister Greer, handling the organization behind it all.

"So Greer is already up at the resort with Noah and Ford," he said, speaking of Greer's husbands.

"I know. They got there last night to make sure it was all set up."

"Well, they're set up there, but it looks like parking's going to be an issue."

I frowned. "It's a resort. How's parking an issue?"

"Because it's set up on the mountains, and the reservation apparently had smaller print when it comes to how many cars we're allowed to bring as one reservation."

I scowled. "Can't we just pay for an extra car?" I asked.

Paisley cleared her throat as she came forward. "You would think so. But no. I have already laid into them because it clearly wasn't on any of the forms we signed but is on their website ten pages deep. So they might've covered their ass there legally. If you want, I can raise a big stink again, but I don't think we're going to be allowed to have the extra car."

I pinched the bridge of my nose. "So what does that mean exactly?" I growled.

"It means we're going to put everything that was in Paisley's car in your car, stuff it to the roof, and you two are driving up together."

Paisley stiffened beside Heath, and I had to wonder if she had known that this was going to be the outcome.

I ran my hands through my hair. "Are we going to be able to fit every single thing that you guys need for your entire lives in just one car?" I asked, my voice only a little bitter.

Heath just raised a brow. "Yes. We'll make it work, but it might make things...sticky." He was doing his best not to point out the fact that neither my ex nor I wanted to deal with a long car ride together, but it seemed we didn't have a choice.

"So why did we need two separate cars to begin with?" I asked, and Paisley just gave me a look.

And then I got it. I was supposed to be bringing Dakota, while Paisley brought her husband. So now, somehow, the two of us were the two single people on this family trip. Therefore, we could fit into one car.

"So we're just going to leave your car here?" I asked instead, not waiting on an answer to my previous question that I clearly didn't need, and Paisley nodded.

"It's not a big deal. I should be able to fit my bags amongst the cars. And on the way there, I'll get some work done." She raised her brow. "If you don't mind driving."

There was an odd tension in the air, and Heath just looked between us, his gaze darting at our volleys.

"I have shit to grade too. Books I need to read for the next curriculum. But sure, you can work." I didn't know why I was making a big deal about this. I didn't *want* to sound like an asshole. Ostensibly, it came naturally.

Paisley sighed, her shoulders dropping. I could have kicked myself, but then I saw the gleam in her eyes. "No, no, no. We can take turns. Anytime that there's a rest stop we'll just jump out while the car's running and pretend that it's not insane."

Heath cursed under his breath. "Okay, okay, I love this whole bickering thing, but I thought you guys were over it. It's going to be a long fucking trip if you guys don't stop it."

"Language!" Devney called out as she strapped Hayleigh into her car seat.

My twin pinched the bridge of his nose. "We're heading out in a few, come on, let's go stuff the bags inside. The kids are already getting strapped in, meaning we are going to be late." Heath wandered off then, and I gave Paisley a look.

"You ready for this?"

Paisley shrugged before giving me an odd look. "Never. I can drive though. If you truly have work to do. I'm sorry, I just assumed you wanted to drive because you always do...or rather, did."

"It's fine." I shook my head, then let out a sigh, finally relaxing a bit. "I got most of it done already. The couple of hours drive up to the mountains isn't going to be a big issue. And it's not like I was planning on grading in the car. I'm sorry. I'm in a mood."

Her lips twitched. "I've been in a mood for a while now. But at least I get to ignore the phone calls while on the road, right?" At that moment, her phone buzzed, and she cringed when she looked down at the readout.

"Who is it?"

"*The Dallas Star.*"

"Why would *the Dallas Star* be calling you? We live in Colorado."

"Jacob's family has business ties there, so evidently, they want an exclusive interview. Not that anyone's getting an exclusive interview."

I cleared my throat. "I didn't realize divorcing Jacob was going to be such a big issue. I mean...press-wise." I needed to take a few lessons in not being an idiot.

She gave another one-armed shrug. "It's just going to get worse." I frowned at her, and she shook her head. "No, I'm not going to dwell on it right now. We have an entire car ride to do that. Come on, the kids are waiting. And we need to empty my car."

I nodded tightly, and I went to move her bags to my vehicle. She didn't have that much, and I figured the only reason we had decided to bring an extra car was so the two of us wouldn't be forced to be in the same car.

And while we could have figured out a way to swap vehicles to the point that I wouldn't have to ride with Paisley, I wasn't about to break up family time for my siblings just because I was forced to drive in a car with my ex-wife.

Soon we were on the road, with me trailing behind the others since Heath liked to be in front, and we had to make sure Luca didn't get left behind because the guy got distracted about everything on the side of the road, and then we were in the quiet, without music or podcasts, as Paisley went to work on her laptop in the passenger seat.

"You can play something. Or listen to a book. I promise I can pay attention to more than one thing."

"I didn't want to bother you," I bit out.

"I just have a few details on this contract to work through. I don't plan on working this entire trip. I don't want to work at all, but things got a little behind with the wave of press and with the sale of the company."

As we drove up the highway, I frowned over at her after going over her words. "You're selling something?"

She nodded tightly. "The matchmaking company. We're almost done with all of the paperwork, but the original owners wanted to try something new, and while they weren't the overall shareholders, I wasn't about to hurt the company by being set in my ways. It's a good move, and it'll make everyone a lot of money. So what could be wrong about it?"

"Probably because selling a matchmaking company

while your divorce is in the news isn't the thing you really want to deal with."

She scowled over me. "I love that everybody seems to be in PR these days."

"What? I read things." Though I'd done my best to ignore any mention of my ex-wife in the news recently.

She snorted. "You do. And the process of selling the company had been going on longer than my divorce. Although it felt like forever for my divorce." She rolled her eyes at that, and I changed lanes, getting out of the way of an eighteen-wheeler that was already having issues with the mountains.

"So, other than Jacob being an asshole, what happened?"

"What happened with Dakota?" she shot right back. "I was surprised not to find her here."

I scowled. "Dakota and I just didn't work out," I said vaguely.

There was no need for her to realize that Dakota had dumped me because she thought I still had feelings for Paisley. Because that couldn't be further from the truth.

"Fine, don't tell me. However, I'm not going to be able to hide why I got a divorce soon. Because Jacob will be marrying the lovely Lydia Samson soon."

My foot revved the engine a bit, and I held onto the

steering wheel, making sure I didn't lose control. "He fucking cheated on you?"

The laugh that escaped her throat was anything but humorous. "Yep. Nearly the whole time. And her family makes a lot more sense than my family as far as who he should be married to. So I don't know why he didn't just marry her to begin with. But no, he wanted to fuck her when he was fucking me over. So yes, soon people will realize that the timeline of his upcoming nuptials are going to be a little too tight for everybody to be happy about it. So now I will not only be the woman who got left behind, I'll be the scorned woman, the other woman."

"I'm pretty sure Lydia would be the other woman."

"Maybe. Or maybe I was just the other woman that he happened to marry for a little while. He thought he could use my money, my business ties, and mold me into the woman he wanted, and it didn't work out. It's fine, Lydia fits him like a glove, a snakeskin one. And they can be happy and take over the world together, and I will just take over the business world, and crush him with my stiletto whenever I can."

Emotions warred within me, at the pride of knowing that she could break him, but anger at the fact that that man had dared to hurt her.

Because in the nonchalance, and her anger woven through it, she was hurt.

And damn it, I didn't want to feel anything.

"I'm sorry."

She shrugged. "Don't be. You didn't do anything."

Yes, I did; I was the one that had started this all, but I wasn't about to make this all about me. Not when this was our family trip, and I needed to get over myself.

"If you want, I could beat him up. But I feel like you should be the one to do that."

Her lips twitched. "That is very true. I've always wanted to kick his ass, but I'm not a violent person."

"You're not. And frankly, I'm not either. I joke about it, but I've never beaten the shit out of someone."

"It sounds like it'd be a lot of work. And then we'd have to deal with icing your hands, because no matter what, you'd still hurt yourself. There are other ways to break a man down though." She winced. "When I'm talking about this, I'm not talking about you. I'd like to think that you and I have found a reasonable middle ground here where we don't hate each other."

"I don't hate you, Paisley," I whispered.

I heard her swallow, before she let out a breath. "I don't hate you either. Sometimes I used to think it would be easier to, but for some reason I'm going on your family vacation, because I love those two women that happened to marry into your family, and Greer is becoming a good friend as well. So, I am fine. Everything is fine."

"Your voice got a little high when you said that."

"It did, didn't it?" she said with a laugh. "I have a couple more emails to deal with, and then I'm going to relax on vacation. With your family."

"The girls are your family too."

"Yes. And I love those nieces of yours."

"They are pretty amazing."

"They have you wrapped around their finger."

"Pretty much. Did you hear that Keelie wanted me to drive her, and no one else?" I said, sounding like a proud uncle.

"I didn't, but I can believe it. Those girls are loved beyond all measure."

"They are. And I'm grateful we all live here to make sure they're never alone. You know?"

"I do. Should I say congratulations on the upcoming happy news?" she asked, and I heard the bitterness mixed with humor in her voice.

That could only mean one thing.

"Let me guess, Devney and Addison mentioned the fact my parents are getting married again even though I thought they were already married."

"I do not understand your parents."

"If you ever do figure them out, let me know because I have no idea what the fuck they are thinking. They're literally insane."

"I don't understand why they would get together after they were divorced. I mean, things were probably said the first time, and they got back together?"

I looked over at her, as I took the exit for the resort.

"If anything, you and I are evidence that people can somehow find a way to create a friendship, if anything, after a divorce." Look at me, sounding all calm and adult like. There was nothing inside of me that was calm at that moment.

"Exactly. We're finding a way, and we're not fighting or bickering at every turn. Look at us, we spent an entire trip up into the mountains so far and we haven't screamed at each other or bickered at all. I call this progress."

"Exactly. And yet, my parents love yelling at each other, to the point it's almost a prelude to them wanting to get married again. At least we're all old enough that once they divorce again and realize that it was all a fucking mistake and there are no such things as second chances, they're not going to try to split up the family again. And we're going to do all that we can to protect those kids. Because my nieces? They're never going to know that Grammy and Grandpa are horrible fucking people. They're only going to know the good things."

Paisley studied my face for a moment, and I couldn't read her expression as I was trying to focus on the road, and then I realized what I had just said.

There were no such things as second chances.

Well, it was the truth, wasn't it? It wasn't as if Paisley and I needed or wanted a second chance.

But maybe second chances could be friendship, there was that at least.

As we wove over the next highway, we were quiet for a bit, as I listened to a book, and she finished up her work. And as we crested over the ridge, the grandeur of the resort in sight, I blinked.

"This place is huge. And they don't have parking?"

"It looks like it. I'll deal with that paperwork later. Because I'm grumpy."

"Enjoy yourself first though, okay?"

"Will do, okay."

We pulled into the visitor parking at first, not knowing exactly where we were supposed to be. Then jumped out of the car to go get our keys for our rooms. The resort wasn't all one big building, it was multiple buildings set into the sides of the mountains to blend in. Some places were little cabanas with mini kitchens, and I knew that Greer and her husband were in one of those, and that's who we were bringing most of the food for. The other buildings were more like hotel and resort rooms, and the way we had booked it, meant that the two families with kids would share a large living room area, a common place so that way they wouldn't have to double up on things for the girls, and Paisley and I would have separate rooms on either side of that.

Or at least that's what I thought.

"What do you mean that's not our reservation?" Paisley asked, her voice icy.

There was something fucking hot about the way her voice slid like sin and frost down my spine.

I needed to get out of that mindset.

"It's just like I said. We have one cabana, and two sets of suites. There are full king beds on either side of the suites, as well as a common area with multiple bathrooms in one, and one main bathroom in the other. This is what the reservation is," the lady was saying, and I didn't like her tone.

My brothers were giving me an odd look, as if judging my reaction, and I wasn't sure what I was supposed to say.

As they went into the details, and Paisley pulled out her printed and digital reservation items, we realized we were getting hosed. It didn't matter what Paisley had on paper, or what we had paid for, we were going to be forced to take what was left or leave.

When Greer and her husband showed up, they joined in the conversation since they had been on the same reservation, and had signed for what we had asked for, and were not getting.

None of it made sense, and all I knew was now we were holding keys, and I was royally fucked.

Because I wasn't going to be sharing a room with Paisley per se, but I was going to be sharing a suite, a bathroom, and a door with my ex-wife.

It was that or splitting up families.

Part of me wanted to sleep on my brother's couch and call it a day, and the rest of me knew I needed to be an adult about the situation and just deal with it.

I truly did not want to have to share a roof with my ex-wife.

Not because I hated her, not because I couldn't stand to be alone with her.

No, the exact opposite.

Because part of me routinely wanted to be alone with her. Part of me missed her.

Part of me wanted her.

And that part was going to have to get with the program. I was going to be sharing a room with my ex-wife.

And there was no way I was going to be able to get out of this.

I met Paisley's gaze, as everyone looked cautiously upon us, and I knew it was going to be a long fucking vacation.

At least there was alcohol. Alcohol would save me.

And I would just pretend that I wasn't going to use it as a crutch. I tried to have resolve, even as I watched Paisley bend down to pick up her bag and told myself it was going to be a really long fucking night.

Chapter Eight

Paisley

I wasn't quite sure why I was even here. The fact I'd not only said yes, but traveled all the way into the mountains with the Cassidys didn't make any sense.

I was just the family friend. The auntie to two beautiful girls, but no longer by familial ties. Maybe if I had stayed married to August all those years ago, I would have been able to truly understand and be connected in that way but that had never been in the cards. Especially when it hadn't been my choice to begin with.

It was odd that I kept thinking about that, that no matter what happened in my life recently, it always came back to August.

Then again it made sense. I was hanging out with his family at a beautiful lodge and resort in the Colorado

Rocky Mountains. And his family was laughing and drinking and eating and just enjoying themselves. And I was doing my best not to act as if I was afraid of what was going to happen next. After all, my life felt as if I were falling into an abyss, and nothing was making sense.

Because August was their uncle, and I was their auntie because I was best friends with their moms. Everything needed to calm down, to slow down. And yet, it was all I could do not to take two steps back and realize that maybe I shouldn't have come.

I had to ask myself exactly why I was sitting here, why I couldn't just pretend like I had always done before.

I sipped my champagne cocktail and watched the two little girls run across the field, with the Cassidy men following them. The guys had their arms up, pretending they were some form of Sasquatch or bear or other terrifying animal, while the little girls screamed and giggled, before they were all tackled to the floor, everybody laughing. Greer was following them, phone in hand as she recorded the moments, and I sat on the lounge deck, drinking away and pretending to relax.

I was never truly good at relaxing honestly.

"So do you want to talk about it?" Addison asked, and I frowned and looked over at my friend. Addison sat on one side of me, Devney the other. I was grateful for the two of them as they stood by me no matter what and had given me time and space after the divorce announcement, but we hadn't talked about it in detail. The distance and lack of delving into the situation was on me, and I needed to worry about what all of this meant. I needed to come to terms with the fact I wasn't up front with my best friends.

My best friends had been amazing, comforting, caring, and not too nosy. However, I knew my time of hiding in my feels when it came to at least Jacob were at an end. After all, there was only so much hiding I could do. It wasn't as if anybody other than August knew why the two of us had been divorced. It had been a subject off limits to everyone, including the two of us. We had never discussed it, and our families had never truly discussed it. Maybe he had with his brothers, I didn't know. I didn't want to know. Perhaps that was bordering on unhealthy, but I didn't care in that moment.

"I assume you're talking about my divorce."

The girls gave each other a look, and I set my drink down. "I meant with Jacob." I pinched the bridge of my nose. "I'm not even thirty years old, and now I've been divorced twice. This isn't exactly where I thought I'd be in my life. I suppose there is no going back to the decisions that I have foisted upon myself."

"Yes. With Jacob." I heard the emphasis on his name and chose to ignore it. "You're away from it all now. Can we do anything for you?" Devney asked, so soft, so caring. She could also stand up for anybody in her life, and I was so grateful for her. Sometimes I felt like I took too much from my friends. I tried to give back, I tried to be a good friend, but I wasn't sure it was enough sometimes.

The effort was on me I knew, but I was trying.

So trying.

"He cheated. He cheated on me, and I walked away. I didn't scream or shout, I just picked up my bag and told him that my lawyer would be contacting his." I downed the rest of my drink, then calmly poured another one since the bottle was right next to me. It was nice they made it so easy like that.

The girls gave me a worried look, and I shook my head.

"I'm not even sad about it." I paused, trying to make sure that that was truly the case and sadly it was. "I'm not sad that I lost him. I realized that as I signed my name on all those papers dissolving our marriage, I didn't love him. I thought I had. I thought I had feelings for him, and I was ready to look into the future and enjoy being someone's wife, but I was wrong." I gulped half of my wine back, then set glass down. "How crazy is that? I thought I could be married. And we all know that that's not the case."

"We don't know anything of the sort. Jacob's an asshole, and he's lucky that he's so far away or I would geld him."

I looked over at Addison. "You wouldn't geld him. He would sue. He has good lawyers. Not as talented as my lawyers, but good lawyers."

"We could just use your good lawyers to get her out of that," Devney said, but I heard the worry in her tone.

"We don't need to geld him. He's out of my life." I winced. "Except for the fact I'm sure that his engagement to his mistress will be in the news soon, and then I'll have to deal with that as well."

"Oh, Paisley."

I shook my head. "I'm fine. Really. And I know that every time I say I'm fine you imagine this black cat with wide eyes and hair all in a hundred different ways, but I swear I'm fine. I am just annoyed with myself for falling for it."

"Well, I'm annoyed for you for not leaning on us or telling us you were getting a damn divorce," Addison snapped.

I stiffened but knew that this was my issue. I was the one who had gotten myself into this situation and I would deal with the consequences.

"I was handling the press, paperwork, and situation."

Devney bit her lip before she spoke. "Alone. You don't have to be that way. We have each other. Yes, we work together, but we're best friends. We should lean on one another in times of strife, happiness, joy, and so much more. You are there for us—no matter what else you have going on in your world. We're here for you too, Paisley."

"I could handle it on my own," I lied, but I could feel the insecurity in my own voice.

"Just because you can doesn't mean you should. I didn't realize you were so unhappy. How selfish were we that we were in our own little lives we didn't realize that you were unhappy." Devney set down her drink and frowned, and I quickly stood up to go to her. When I knelt beside her, Addison came over and sat down and lounged next to Devney, but not to block me out, more so it was at the three of us. Like it should have been this whole time.

"I didn't want to be a failure. I didn't want to be the twice divorced woman in her late twenties, not even thirty or forty wondering why she can't make it work. I just wanted to throw it under the rug and watch you guys thrive. There's been so much going on in your lives and I've loved being a part of it. I just didn't want you to have to deal with mine."

"You're allowed to be less than perfect. And if anything, it seems like he was the imperfect one," Devney said.

"Far from perfect for either one of us."

"We're allowed to take the good and the bad. You've helped us through so much. Hell, you saved me after I thought everything was ruined with my last job."

"Your last job didn't appreciate you. I do." I waved that off like it didn't matter, but when she pinched my side, I frowned.

"Hey, what was that for?"

"Stop making your strides trivial. You saved me."

"Me too. You helped me figure out exactly who I needed to be. And both of us can be moms and wives and women and business-oriented people. We're able to do it all, and yet still have a vacation together because you found a way to make it happen. And I'm sorry that Jacob's an asshole, but he was never good enough for you."

"He wasn't. I thought he was. I thought he was nice."

"He was. At least he seemed it. And I'm sorry we didn't see beneath that surface," Addison said as she squeezed my hand.

"Well, he's gone. And I'm going to have another drink, and I'm not even going to think about him again. Because that's why I'm here with you. On a vacation with the family that's not my own, I'm going to have a drink, watch you guys play with your families and thrive and be wonderful. And then I'll deal with the press and the fallout and everything that comes from that man later."

The girls gave me a look, and we continued to talk, and I knew that no matter what I said, I would still have to grovel a bit more.

I should have told them. I knew it. But I'd been so embarrassed.

I had wanted to make this marriage work. I couldn't make mine with August work, but maybe I could have made one with Jacob work. On paper we fit in every way possible. And then he had left me just like August had.

And on that thought, I took another drink, once again annoyed with myself.

By the time we had dinner, I was a few drinks in, but didn't switch to water. I wasn't slurring or messy, but I was quiet, eating while everybody laughed and joked and talked about the next day's activities, while I nodded along and ate my food. August kept giving me weird looks, but then again, he always did. So far, we were making the room situation work, however, this would be our first night sleeping under the same roof. Well, not the exact first night considering I'd slept in his guest room not too long ago. I would just pretend it was that. Another way of me making a fool of myself. Oh look, another drink.

When I switched to water, August looked less concerned, and I wanted to go do shots or something just to annoy him. But that was petty, and I was not petty.

I was just tired.

And alone. But I was better off alone. Getting messy with anyone else just felt like connections that didn't make any sense.

I wasn't going to let that be a problem.

Instead, when everyone moved off to the cabana to watch a movie, I waved them off and went to my room.

I would go take a bath, have some alone time while they had family time.

Because they had made families. And I, the person who was ahead of the game, was far behind.

Go me.

I went to my bathroom and turned on the faucet, letting the water pour and fill up the tub, while I went to pour myself a glass of wine.

"Shouldn't you have some more water?"

I nearly dropped the glass, fumbling it in my hand, as wine sloshed over the side.

"What the hell?" I snapped, setting the bottle down. "I could have broken that."

"You didn't. Good reflexes for someone who's wasted."

"I'm not wasted. I'm buzzed. I'm happy. Let me be happy."

He gave me a look and shook his head. I could never read that look. Maybe I used to at one point, but then again, I hadn't been good at that before, had I?

"You were just fine at reading my looks before," he growled.

Maybe I'd had too much to drink if I had said that out loud and I hadn't realized.

"Why are you here? Shouldn't you be with your family?"

"My family is hanging out with the kids and having child movie time. Greer and her husbands are off in their cabin alone and I don't want to think about that. So I was going to sit in the living room or take a hot shower. Except you are in my bathroom."

I pointed the wine bottle at him. "My bathroom. I'm going to take a bath, read a book, and finish this bottle of wine."

"Great, so you're going to be in here, taking up the time and space, while I have nowhere to go to be alone."

"You have the entire resort. I'm sure there's some single woman you can go slough off with and go have fun. Make a party of it. There's a hotel bar."

He narrowed his eyes at me. "That's just catty. You're not catty, Paisley."

I sighed and drained my partially filled glass. "I'm not catty. So I'm sorry. I just wanted to relax and take a bath. Have some alone auntie time. While everyone's off enjoying themselves."

"Paisley," he whispered, taking a step.

I set down the glass and scrambled back, hands in front of me.

"Don't. Don't pity me. I'm not pitying *you* for being here alone." I cursed under my breath. "Not that I should. There's nothing wrong with being alone. That's what I keep telling myself. Ms. Twice-divorced."

"Paisley," he repeated.

"I hate when you say my name." A falsehood.

"You didn't always."

I narrowed my gaze at him, wondering what the hell he was on about. Then I realized that he had been matching me drink for drink.

I pointed at him, mouth agape. "You're drunk too."

"That means if I'm drunk as well, that means you're drunk. It's science and semantics."

"Get better at the cutting remarks. Mr. I'm Drunk But I'm Going to Yell at You for Being Drunk."

"I'm not drunk, I'm just happy."

"You're not happy, August. But it's okay, you can have some of my wine. I'll be charitable."

"I've been drinking bourbon, switching to wine sounds like a hangover. I'm not in my early twenties anymore."

I winced at that, remembering that no, we were not in our early twenties anymore.

If anything, thirty was hitting us quickly. On our next birthdays.

I shuddered at that, and went to check the temperature of the water, adjusting the taps a bit.

"Are you cold?"

I shook my head. "No, I was just thinking about the fact I'm turning thirty soon. Which isn't old, but it is an age that happens to be a milestone. A milestone that I'm apparently not ready for."

He frowned at me. "What do you mean you're not ready for?"

I pointed at him, annoyed. "I am not where I thought I would be."

"An uber successful businesswoman who is literally on the *Forbes* list right now? The one who young girls actually look up to, and I have actually seen one dress up as you for Halloween one year in my high school."

I blinked at him. "What?"

He waved it off. "No, never mind. Don't want to inflate your ego."

"Someone dressed up as me for Halloween?" I asked, my voice going slightly high-pitched.

"Yeah. You hit the *Forbes* list. One of my students wants to be a female CEO who takes over the world. You're happening to do it before anyone else, so when everyone was allowed to dress up on Halloween, she was you. I thought it was hilarious."

"And she didn't realize that you knew me?" I asked, incredulously.

"Nope. Yes, PCR is the name of the company, but nobody connects the Cassidy to us."

I cringed. "I regretted putting the C in there, not because it was you," I said, wondering why I was apologizing to him for divorcing me. "Mostly because when Devney and then Addison got married and changed their names, people started to wonder."

"I'd say I'm sorry about people wondering, but then again, I don't think I have enough booze for everything that we'd need to unpack from that conversation."

I snorted, then turned off the taps. "August. There's not enough booze for any of this."

"I'm glad Jacob's not here."

I blinked, swallowing hard. The energy in the room had shifted, and I had to wonder if I'd had too much to drink at this point. No, my reflexes were still there. But something had changed.

"Why? Dakota seemed nice." There. That was gracious.

He shook his head. "Yeah. Too nice for me."

"You are nice too, August. Even when you're an asshole."

"That doesn't make any sense, Paisley."

"It doesn't have to make any sense. I just want to drink my wine in peace."

"And take over my bathroom?" he asked, moving closer.

"Our bathroom. Mine for now."

"So you think you can just get naked in our bathroom, sink into bubbles, and pretend I don't fucking care?"

The glass nearly fell out of my hands, and he took it from me, setting in on the counter.

"What are you talking about, August?"

"I'm going to do something that's going to be a really big fucking mistake."

"August."

Before I could say anything else, his mouth was on mine, and I was letting it happen. Without hesitation.

Somehow his hands were pulling on my robe, and I was tugging on his shirt, his taste bursting on my tongue.

It was odd to think that his taste was so familiar, and yet so different.

Because I had married this man. He had been my first, my first everything. I had let him kiss and touch every inch of my body.

But in this moment, he wasn't that person. Nor was I the same woman as before. This was familiar and yet new. And this was such a mistake. A mistake I didn't hate.

But I was so tired, so tired of being alone, pretending I didn't want someone to touch me.

So I let him.

And when he ran his lips down my jaw, I arched my chin up so he could lick down my neck, sucking and tasting. When my robe fell to the floor, cool air slid over my skin, my nipples pebbling, goosebumps washing over my flesh.

"Paisley, you're so fucking beautiful."

"Just don't talk," I whispered.

He raised a brow at me.

"Really?"

"Not right now. Because then I'll remember how wrong this is. How we shouldn't be doing this."

"You're right. I won't talk. I just need a taste."

And then he was on his knees, and his mouth was on my pussy.

I clenched, my hands gripped the side of the sink, and my knees went weak as he licked at my pussy, spreading me.

His dark hair between my legs was the most erotic thing I had ever seen, and my knees nearly buckled completely. But he kept me steady, nibbling on my flesh, before taking one hand to spread me more, using the other hand to play along my clit.

He ate and licked like he was a man starving, and when he speared me with two fingers, curling them just in the way he remembered, I couldn't control myself, I came, my cunt clamping down on his fingers as he continued to lave at me, licking up my juices.

His beard was rough on my skin, and I knew he would leave a mark, but I wanted his mark. I wanted a memory of this moment even though I knew I should probably forget.

The orgasm shocked through me, my toes curling, my nipples hardening to stiff points. And then he was on his feet again, crushing his mouth to mine. I could taste myself on him, tart and sweet, and I groaned, pulling at his shirt. He tossed it over his head, and then I was pulling down his gray sweatpants, grateful he hadn't bothered to put on underwear.

I had already been able to see the tip of him poking out above the waistband, and so when I gripped the base of his shaft, he groaned, pumping into my hand.

"I need you," he groaned.

I wanted that to mean more, and yet it couldn't mean more. I wouldn't let it mean more.

So I nodded and let him pull me on top of the sink. And when I spread my legs, he sank into me in one thrust. Hard and fast and unyielding.

I let out a shocked gasp at the intrusion, my pussy fluttering around his dick.

"Oh!" I whispered.

He froze, his forehead resting on my shoulder as he kept me steady.

"Too hard? Did I hurt you?"

The break in his voice at that nearly sent me into tears, but I didn't want to think about that. I couldn't.

"No, just a surprise. Please move."

"I'm sorry."

"I meant in me. Fuck me, August. Please."

He smiled then, that sweet and annoying fucking smile of his. "Look at that, Paisley begging."

"I already got off, August. So if you're just going to

stand there, you can, but I can get myself off again." I winked as I said it, sliding my hand over my clit. He took my wrist and pulled my hand back, before thrusting in and out of me.

"No, your orgasm is mine."

My eyes widened. "Excuse me."

He kissed me hard, then leaned down and bit my nipple. The sharp sting sent waves of pleasure down to my core.

"You heard me. Your orgasm is mine. Your pussy is mine. Just for now. I'm going to fuck it all night, and you're going to take it."

"Well, if you insist."

This was the August I remembered. Hard and fast with that playful little smile. And so he slid deep into me, and then he was pulling out, and my feet were on the ground, and then I was facing the mirror. I gripped the edge of the counter again, and he slammed into me from behind. I met his gaze in the mirror, my mouth parting as an orgasm washed over me, but he kept moving, hands on my hips. My hair flew around, bouncing with each thrust, and he kept moving with a bruising force that was the most pleasurable touch I'd ever had in my life.

And when he came, he held me close, hands on my breasts, body touching mine, and a single tear slid down my cheek. I wiped it away before he could see it in the reflection, and then he pulled out, and we were kissing, and then we were in the tub, water splashing over the edge as he cleaned me, and then licked me, and then came inside me again.

I let him hold me, knowing that we would have to talk about this at some point.

And somehow, I found myself in his arms in the tub, letting him hold me, neither one of us speaking.

And yet for one moment, for this exact moment in time, I could breathe again. I could feel.

And this overwhelming feeling of calm, of contentedness, worried me more than any other mistake I had made in my life.

Chapter Nine

August

This time when I went to take a shower, Paisley wasn't there, and I was grateful for her absence. I turned on the faucet, water falling from the rain showerhead, and I stuck my hand under it, grateful it was ice-cold. When I stepped underneath the flowing water, I gritted my teeth, bearing the ice-cold temperature as I tried to clear my head.

Too much drink, too many poor decisions, and not enough brainpower had led to what had happened.

Everything had been a terrible mistake, but it wasn't as if we could take it back. Or perhaps I could lie and pretend, but I didn't think so. And I wasn't sure I wanted to either.

I quickly ran a washcloth over my body, using whatever soap that happened to be in the shower. It smelled like citrus and maybe a little coconut, and figured I would smell like a tropical drink the rest of the day but I didn't care.

Part of me wanted to wash Paisley's scent off me, the rest wanted to keep it. But then I remembered how her hair had smelled like this earlier, because she had probably used it when she had showered before.

So now I was going to smell like her anyway, despite the fact that I was trying to scrape off any semblance of the mistakes I had made the night before.

I had been the one to pursue her. To want to kiss her, the one to fuck her on the countertop. Yes, she had leaned in, had taken, had wanted as much as I had.

But I had made the first move.

I had been the one to step across the line after so many years of not doing so. Of staying away because it would be safer if I did.

So I was to blame.

And I didn't have a good reason for any of it, other than the fact that I wanted her.

And I had wanted her for far too long.

I finished showering and turned off the water, getting out while wrapping a towel around my waist.

When I looked up, I realized I wasn't alone.

Paisley stood in the doorway—her hair tousled as if someone had been running their hands through it all night. Well, that someone had been me. I had been the one to take her, to want her, and to not give a flying fuck about the consequences.

What the hell had I been thinking?

She looked like a damn goddess, wrapped in that white robe that had come with the room, her lips swollen from the night before. She had such a look of innocence in her eyes, weariness. That was on me though. We had done so well about not making poor choices all these years, and then here we were, making them again.

I was a damn asshole.

I had done my best to never fall in love with Paisley over these years we'd been apart. Or at least never to admit that I had fallen in love with her. No, that wasn't right. It was all about admitting that I still loved her. That I had walked away because of that love, however selfish that may be.

And now here she stood, in our shared bathroom, looking lost.

Perhaps just as lost as I felt.

"Do you need the shower?" I grunted, while I took a step to the side and gestured toward it. "It's all yours. There's plenty of hot water."

She frowned at me then, but I didn't rise to the bait,

didn't do anything other than stand there and watch her try to think.

My beautiful, sweet Paisley who wasn't mine. She was eternally on her toes, thinking faster than the rest of us, and smarter than all of us combined. Then I had broken her brain.

I was a damn asshole.

"Yeah, a shower would be good." She cleared her throat, that smokiness that had come from either disuse, or screaming my name too loudly in the night making her voice sound husky as hell.

My dick hardened at the thought, which was surprising considering how many times I had come the night before. I hadn't thought my dick had it in him. So I turned so the rise of my towel didn't cause any attention and walked through her bedroom to the living room. Because I had not wanted to stand there any longer, nor be forced to walk past her into her bedroom. Because we hadn't used the two rooms. Instead we had used my bed.

I was such a damn idiot.

I walked through the shared living room, and into my bedroom once I heard the bathroom door close. The sound of water reached my ears, and I was grateful that she had turned the shower on.

I didn't want to think about her naked in there,

water sluicing down those beautiful curves of hers. But here I was, being the maker of my own mistakes.

I dropped the towel, and pulled on my clothes, figuring jeans and a Henley would have to do for the day. I could work, I could look at lesson plans, I could read a book, I could go on a fucking hike. I could do anything but stand in this room that smelled of sex and Paisley and wonder exactly what I was going to do once she got back here.

I didn't have any other answers.

What was I supposed to be thinking in this moment other than the fact that I had just slept with my ex-wife.

Multiple times.

And part of me, most of me, wanted to do it again.

The logical part of me that knew that nothing good could come of this knew I should probably run. Head home and make up an emergency.

No good could come from sleeping with my ex-wife again.

As the water turned off, I let out a breath, knowing my time had run out. Only she didn't open the door. Instead I heard her moving around in there, probably getting ready, probably putting on the shield that she wore so well so nobody could see beneath it.

Once I had had the pleasure of doing so. The responsibility of being that person.

Now she was hiding. Just like I was.

I moved out to the living room, and looked for my shoes, figuring I should leave before she got out here.

Then her bedroom door opened into the living room, and Paisley stood there, her hair wet but scrunched into her natural waves.

She hadn't put on makeup but had put on linen pants and a soft peach-colored shirt along with a cardigan that covered most of her up.

She looked gorgeous, younger, and hesitant.

And I had put that look on her face.

"I am going to head down, find something to eat. Then see what the family's up to."

There, I sounded like a human. Like I knew what I was doing. I found my shoes and stuffed my feet in them, but Paisley didn't move forward.

"I can go pick up something in a bit. I'll let you leave first."

I held back a smirk at that, because of course we couldn't be seen together after what happened the night before. Even though everyone knew we'd shared the suite together, I was afraid they'd know *exactly* what we'd done once they saw us together for the first time. And while I didn't care, or at least I told myself I didn't care, I did.

I didn't know why I was annoyed at the concept. It

wasn't as if I wanted anything more from her. I needed to be the one who left. And I was grateful she didn't want to come with me. Because then we would have to talk.

And on that note. "We're not going to talk about it."

My back was to her, but I still heard the intake of breath, but not surprise. No, that was anger. Good. Be angry with me. Hate me.

That would make all of this so much easier.

"Never again then. Got it. We won't talk about it."

My shoulders tightened, and I finally turned to her, seeing a familiar anger on her face. I had done that to her before, and I seem to be good about doing it now. But this was to protect her. She was already going through enough hell, and sleeping with me, being near me, wasn't going to help anything.

"Fine," I bit out.

"By the way, I was on birth control. And I'm clean. I had to do multiple checks after I found out Jacob was cheating." Her left eye twitched slightly, her jaw tightening, and I closed my eyes, pinching the bridge of my nose.

"Fuck. I didn't even think."

"No. You didn't. I did, but then I realized that I was clean, and I was on birth control, and we were just going to wing it because that's what we're good at doing. I hope you're clean."

I nodded. "I am. I just had my yearly physical. And well, I always use condoms."

Except with Paisley. But I didn't need to say that out loud.

She gave me a tight nod. "Fine. Well, if you're going to stand there, I'm going to be the one that leaves first. I think it's only right."

And with that cutting remark, she pushed past me, and closed the door quietly behind her, that little snick echoing in my ears.

Well, I guess that made sense. I had been the one to leave first last time. It was her turn now.

I rubbed my temples, telling myself that we would be able to move on, to ignore all of this and just pretend it hadn't happened.

I could still smell her on my skin and taste her on my tongue. I knew that my bite marks were all over her body, little bruises of tenderness and heat.

I had a horrible feeling that neither one of us were going to be able to forget this.

I left the room finally, grateful that I didn't see any of the women or kids in the central area where food was set up. In fact, I only saw my brothers there, not even Greer or her husbands were about.

"Hey," Luca said, a brow raised.

Heath didn't say anything. Instead he just studied my face and shook his head.

My stomach tightened, but I didn't say anything.

"Where is everyone?" I asked, my voice sounding like I had swallowed gravel. I moved past them to the breakfast bar and began to pile on eggs and bacon. Maybe enough food and grease would help this hangover—the emotional kind—and the fact I had way too much to drink the night before. At some point I had sipped champagne out of Paisley's belly button, and that hadn't gone off well.

Well, we both had gotten off, but now my headache and memories weren't going to go away anytime soon.

"Where's everyone else?" I asked, as I took a seat next to my brothers, and began to shovel in food.

"Greer and her guys are out on a hike, while our wives, Paisley, and the kids, are down at the park. They wanted some fresh air."

There was something in their tone that made me stiffen. "Sounds fun." I wasn't sure what I was supposed to say about that.

"You want to tell us what happened last night?" Heath bit out, and I slowly looked up, letting my fork rest gently on my plate.

"I don't know, what happened last night?"

My brothers looked at each other, then at me.

"How about the fact that we stopped by your room to check on you, and clearly heard what was going on."

I swallowed hard, suddenly not hungry anymore.

"What? What the hell were you doing outside my room?"

"We were checking on you guys because we hadn't heard from you in a while, and when the two of us went by your room, we heard it all. Everything," Heath snapped.

"I don't know why you think it's your business what the hell I do in my own room."

"So you're not denying you fucking slept with Paisley last night?" Luca asked incredulously.

"What I do in the privacy of my room on vacation has nothing to do with you. I don't need to deny or confirm anything."

"I don't want you to get hurt." Heath shook his head, as I blinked at him. "Yes, we love Paisley too and we don't want her to get hurt, but you're our brother. What the hell were you two thinking?"

"I'm still not sure why it's your business?" I bit out.

But for some reason, the fact that my brothers were worried about me, and not just Paisley, hit me odd. I thought they would've been angry that I would have taken advantage of Paisley like that, but they didn't want *me* to get hurt. I couldn't get hurt. I was the one that had broken her to begin with the first time. I was the asshole here. Didn't they see that?

No, they didn't. Because they didn't know what had happened all those years ago. Because I was such a selfish pig, I had hidden everything in the past and did my best to never talk about it. And they were still walking on eggshells around me.

As always.

I didn't deserve their concern.

"It happened once, we had too much to drink, it won't happen again. We already talked about it." Well, saying that we weren't going to talk about it maybe counted as talking about it, and I wasn't going to get too into that. "In the end, it happened, it won't happen again, and we're going to move on. Got it? We're moved on."

"Really? That's what you're going with." Luca shook his head. "What the hell happened, August, before and now?"

I opened my mouth to say something, then realized I didn't have anything to say. Instead I just let out a breath. "I don't know. Either time. But it doesn't matter. It's all in the past."

"Is it?" Heath asked, but before I could say anything, the sound of the children filled the room, and then everybody was there, including Greer and her husbands. Suddenly I had one of my nieces in my lap, and she was telling me about her day as she stole a piece of bacon. I laughed, and ate around her, as everybody moved in, eating snacks and talking about the upcoming plans for the day. Paisley was on the other side of the room, her coffee in hand, as she spoke to Greer, looking as if she hadn't a care in the world.

But I saw the rigid lines of her shoulders, as well as the slight bruise right underneath the edge of her shirt. The bruises that had come from my mouth.

I had done that to her. But we were both good at pretending that nothing had happened. It's what we'd been doing ever since I had moved back to town. I wasn't quite sure what else I was supposed to do about that. How we were supposed to fix it.

"Okay, so moving on again for tonight?" Devney asked as she looked at her planner. "It's a little cloudy, so I don't know if we can do a full star search."

I smiled at that, as the girls leaned into me and Luca, both wanting to see the stars, but wanting to see the latest Disney Princess movie as well.

All I knew was that I would be hanging with my family, not alone, not drinking, and sure as hell without Paisley. Nothing good could come from that.

We were just getting ready to head out, as other

resort guests flowed in and out of the room, when the doors opened, and a familiar voice screeched down my ears, and I had to wonder if I had truly gone to hell and hadn't found my way back.

"Babies, Grammy is here!" my mother said as she moved forward, my father right behind her.

The girls scrambled off our laps, and ran to their grandparents, not knowing that Grammy and Grandpa had not been invited and hadn't been told about this trip.

I looked at my brothers, as well as Greer, and realized they were just as shocked as I was.

When I met Paisley's gaze, I saw the pity there, maybe the confusion.

As my parents couldn't help but go into wedding details, and how they were so happy to surprise us on our family trip so the family could all be there—emphasis on family—I just knew that it would be best if I remembered this exact moment.

My parents were so manically in love in this moment, they didn't care about anyone else except for being the center of attention. Maybe they had shifted slightly over the past couple of years with the arrival of their granddaughters, but not enough in my eyes. They continued to jerk our emotions around as they filled their own wells.

They were the shining examples of what happened when you couldn't make up your mind and continued to fall in and out of love. Because second chances might work for some, but they didn't work for our family. It just fucked everything up for everyone else involved.

I pulled my gaze away from Paisley and told myself that last night would never happen again. It couldn't.

I had watched my parents become exes and then husband and wife before.

I was not going to repeat their mistakes.

So I would never fall in love with my ex-wife again. I would never be with her. And I would never toy with the lives and emotions of those that I loved.

I refused to become my parents.

Even if I hurt the woman that I craved more than anything in the process. It would be good for her in the end.

It had to be.

Chapter Ten

Paisley

I t had been over a week since I had decided to throw caution to the wind and sleep with my ex-husband. That meant it had also been a week since I had spoken to anyone about it.

To say I was an idiot would be an understatement. But it wasn't as if I could go back and fix that. Not when I couldn't not sleep with him. There was no erasing those memories or actions. I had to come to terms with the fact that I had not only orgasmed multiple times with him, but I had also begun to feel something again.

I had loved the August from my past. The one who had cherished me for those few months into a year. The one that I had loved and given myself to. I had loved him and given him everything. And then I had hated him and had been found wanting.

Now as I sat in my office, my large windows behind me and beside me in my corner, because I was the big boss so I got the best space, I had to realize that there was nothing for me to look out upon. There was no future along that path when it came to August. We had gotten drunk, made a mistake, and there would be no consequences from that action.

We weren't going to talk about it, and no one else would ever have to know. We would move on, and I would be the fun aunt to those little babies and any other babies that came to the family. Maybe I would move on one day—never getting married, of course. I would not be getting married three times in my life, thank you very much. But I could find a charming gentleman caller who I could spend evenings with and travel with, and then go home alone so that way I didn't have to share my space with anyone who didn't respect me or didn't know or understand the future that I wanted.

It sounded like a perfect middle ground.

Because it wouldn't be with Jacob or August. Or anyone else who made me feel like I wasn't good enough.

I nearly snapped the pen in half, popping off the lid, and realized that perhaps I was a little more wound up than I had previously thought.

"Knock, knock."

I looked up at the sound of Addison's voice, relieved that I didn't have to wallow further in my own self-pity and memories. Instead I focused on my two best friends as they walked inside, notebooks in hand. Two more staff members came with them, and I raised a brow.

"Was I missing a meeting?"

"Oh no," Addison said, as she handed over a file, and Devney did the same. I took them from her, and nodded at Sarah and Courtney, two other senior staff.

"So no meeting, you just all decided to come at once?"

Courtney laughed and handed over another file, while Sarah did the same.

"No, we were just all on our way to you with things that you needed, and we decided to all step in at the same time rather than taking turns," Devney said, slightly blushing. "Plus you weren't on the phone, and your assistant said you didn't have any more meetings tonight. Just admin work. So we're here to add more to your plate."

"You love us," Addison said, and everyone laughed, including me.

"I do. But now I'm going to be working late into the night. Thank you."

"I'm sorry," Courtney said as she moved forward

with her hand reaching out. "I can take that back and you can work on it another day." I put my hand over the stack of files and shook my head. "No, I can handle it and I promise I won't be here too late. Were these each of the files that we had already been discussing?" I asked, looking at all of them.

Everyone but Addison nodded, and I raised a brow at her.

"This is the file that I was going to turn in next week, but I got things done early. Apparently even I can work on vacation," she replied.

I rolled my eyes as the others laughed. "You say that as if it's a surprise that you worked at all. Though I'm not quite sure how that happened."

"There was a day by the pool. I can't help it. The paperwork was just right there and it was calling to me."

"You're an addict," Devney put in.

Courtney and Sarah waved, and I nodded in acknowledgment as they said their goodbyes, heading back to work, and then I was left alone with my two best friends.

"Well, you aren't the only one that worked on vacation, so thank you for getting this to me early, but you are going to the bottom of the pile."

"No worries. I could have waited, but I figured if you had time, you could fit it into your schedule. I have a thousand other things to do, because spreadsheets don't wait for the weary."

"I feel like you need that on a mug."

"I do love spreadsheets. They make me whole."

"Not your husband or child?" I asked dryly.

"Oh, they do too," Addison said with a wave of her hand. "But spreadsheets? They are what truly give me purpose in life."

She sounded so serious for a moment I was worried that she meant it, before she burst out laughing, and I rolled my eyes toward Devney.

"She's ridiculous."

"Yes, but she's our ridiculous friend."

"Anyway, thank you for the paperwork." I didn't say it too dryly, but Devney just grinned.

"I do love the fact that we get our work done, and it just makes more work for you. But that's why I'm in PR. I just clean up messes, while you organize things." She paused. "Actually, that might be the other way round."

"I really don't mind. I like files." I hesitated for a moment. "Okay, that made me sound like I have no life, but maybe that's true."

I shook my head, as Devney cringed.

"You have a life. With us. I'm sorry, but you're going to have to deal with us for the rest of your life."

"That is very true."

I smiled at my friends, feeling a little guilty that I hadn't told them about August. I was such an idiot. But I should have. I should have told them that I had slept with their brother-in-law and would never speak to him about it again. They already knew about the fact that I had spent the night at his house when I had gotten too drunk. They had yelled at me for that, and I didn't blame them. Mostly because I hadn't called them for help, wanting to handle things on my own. But I was good at taking care of myself. At least that's what I thought.

Addison opened her mouth to say something, but before she could continue, my mother walked in.

Dread settled in my gut, and I stood up, grateful I was wearing my stilettos so I could look as if I were statuesque, a pillar of strength, porcelain that would not shatter.

"Paisley, I have a plan. Get these two out of here. We need to save your marriage. I will not be the laughingstock of society because you can't keep a man."

Embarrassment crawled over me, as Addison glowered at my mother, and Devney looked to me as if she wanted to help but wasn't sure how.

Well same here, I didn't know how to fix this either.

"Mother, this is my place of business. You need to go."

"I will not. I will not let you ruin your life like this. I have a plan to get you back with Jacob, and all of this will be brushed under the rug. You won't need to work at this little job of yours, and deal with these people." She snarled the word people as she looked between Addison and Devney, and I was done. So done with this woman.

I walked around my desk, my stilettos tapping against the marble floors.

"You need to get out of here right now."

"Don't you dare talk to me this way."

"Do not embarrass me at my place of business. I own this place. I am the law here. And I will call security to have you escorted out of here. And those women that you just snarled at? They are not only brilliant women who have high positions in this company and make it work, they are my friends. They deserve to be here, you do not."

"I gave up everything to get you where you are, and this is how you show how grateful you are? You are a spoiled brat and you do not deserve anything that you have. But no matter how many sacrifices I made, I will continue to make them so you can keep your husband."

"He's not my husband. And frankly, you never gave me anything but pain and heartache. Now you will lower your voice before the rest of the building hears you. Or you can continue to scream, and I will have security escort you out and the papers will hear about *your* little tantrum. Is that what you want, Mother?"

"You are a selfish bitch."

She reached out to slap me again, but instead I took a step back and shook my head. "Not again. Never again. Addison, can you hand me my phone? I left it on the desk. I'm going to need to call Jonathan." Jonathan was the head of security and would have my mother out of here in a wink—something I should have done long ago.

"With pleasure."

"You selfish brat. But don't worry, I will fix this."

"There's nothing to fix. Stop acting as if you're in some melodrama. None of this is your business, and the marriage is over. We're divorced. Now, this is my place of business. We are helping people. I'm not going to help you do whatever selfish thing you want."

People were starting to notice now, and I could feel heat rising up my neck.

"Go. Or I will be the one who makes a scene."

My mother studied my face for a moment before she shook her head, clucking her tongue, and walked away with her chin held high as if it was her decision.

I closed the door behind her, needing a moment. My hands shook, my chest squeezing.

"Oh, Paisley. I'm so sorry." Devney reached out and put her hand on my back, and I let out a shuddering breath.

Addison let out a mutter of curses, before coming to my side as well. She wrapped her arm around my waist and then let out a breath.

"I'm sorry that you had to see that. It's nothing new. She liked my station with Jacob because it allowed her to be at a higher place in society as well. She got to meet the governor." I rolled my eyes, before I moved away from my friend and went over to my sideboard to pour myself some water.

"Thirsty?"

"We're fine," Devney whispered behind me. "Is she always like that?"

I took a sip of water, letting myself calm down. "Yes. Has been since I was a child. She hated August. Hated the fact that he was just a schoolteacher. In her eyes, he was a nobody. She didn't see the fact that he worked his ass off and his kids loved him. So she was grateful when that marriage ended. But with Jacob? All of her well-laid plans burst into flames when he chose Lydia over me."

"Your mother's a bitch," Addison said, and I burst out laughing.

"She is. And it's taken me forever to learn how to stand up for myself to her." I looked at my friends, shaking my head. "I can stand up to any businessperson. I stood up to Jacob. I can take care of myself and the people in my employ. But my mother walks in, and suddenly I'm a teenager again, hunching my shoulders and scared of what she could possibly say. I've continuously been a disappointment to her, even with everything that I've done, and it's never going to be enough for her. I should just be used to it, but I don't know, something about the way that she looks down at me, even though I'm taller than her, gets to me and I'm suddenly a child again."

"She's so wrong about you. You should be proud of all that you've done. And Jacob was never worthy of you. He was always a jerk."

I narrowed my gaze at Devney. "And yet no one told me that."

"Because he hid it well, and we thought you loved him. Next guy you date, we'll tell you if he's an asshole or not," Addison said, but both of my friends' eyes were watery.

I finished my water and let out a long sigh. "I have to get back to work. But I'm sorry you had to witness that."

"I'm sorry it seems that you've dealt with that often alone," Devney whispered.

"What she said," Addison agreed.

I nodded tightly, and then watched them walk away, leaving me alone with my paperwork.

My paperwork never lied to me—most of it was just numbers and signatures. I could handle that, go over it with a fine-tooth comb, and then head home alone where I needed to be.

I didn't know exactly what plans my mother had, and I had a bad feeling about some of them. But I would figure them out. I would *always* figure it out.

I went back to work, and as the sun began to set, I kept the shades open, so that way the world could see the light on in my office and know that I was still up here. Working, never going home.

Others left, and my security team was still around, though they weren't watching me like a hawk. Instead they kept the building safe, and I would have to go home soon so that way they could get off work. It would be selfish to continue to stay here when they had lives.

I packed up the rest of my files; I knew I would go home and take care of it, maybe pour a glass of wine, maybe take that bath I hadn't gotten to before. And I would continue to just exist.

"Paisley."

I looked up at the sharp tone, my hands balling into fists.

"What are you doing here, Jacob?" I asked,

wondering why today felt like I had been thrown into another vat of hell. First my mother, now my ex-husband? Why did this feel like a trap?

"You didn't sign the non-disclosure. I need you to do that."

I raised a brow, wondering what size balls this man thought he had. "No, I'm not going to sign anything. We've already done everything over the divorce, the settlement is done. I'm not signing your silly little non-disclosure."

"You will. You are no longer my wife, and you will sign it outside of the umbrella."

The umbrella, AKA, the family. You know, whatever protected them from the onslaught of truths and deniers.

"No, I'm not going to sign anything. And I'm not going to get sued by you if you think that I've spilled some form of rumor about you. Because, Jacob darling, once news of your tiny dick gets out there and the lovely cheating scandals, you're going to want a fall guy. And it's not going to be me. You don't get to sue me because you cheated on me."

Jacob was in front of me in an instant, caging me around my desk.

I had never seen him move that quickly. Usually he was smooth grace, and fluid. But just then and there, the jerky actions nearly took my breath away. He caught me between his arms on the desk, and I swallowed hard, staring up into his face.

"Say that again to my face, Paisley. You were such a frigid bitch when I was with you it took forever to thaw you out, and you were never a good lay. Why do you think I was with Lydia? Oh, it doesn't matter what you think, it only matters what the press says. And while you would love to think my family controls the press, you know that isn't the case. We have our ways to make our mark—to keep our *legacy*, and this is one of them. So you're going to sign this non-disclosure, and you're going to do what I say, or I'm going to make life hell for you."

"Try it," I snapped, yet I knew I was only playing with fire. Because I had never truly felt safe with Jacob, not that first night, not any night since. But right here and now, I knew I was alone in the office, and I didn't know where my security was.

"Bitch," Jacob snapped, leaning forward.

I stepped back, but he was fast, lunging toward me, arms outstretched. He gripped my upper arm, his fingers digging into my skin, and I pulled way. Only he was stronger than I remembered and while I tried to think beyond the heartbeat rattling in my ears, I shoved at him.

As Jacob moved me closer to my desk, trying to push

me down along the hard wood, I kicked and ignored the panic in my veins.

Then he was being pulled off of me, and I was trying to catch my breath.

August was there, shaking out his fists, after a loud smack hit my ears. Jacob howled, covering his nose, and August glowered at the man.

"Touch her again, and I'll kill you."

"Fuck you."

"Oh, that's brilliant. Lovely retort. Why don't you get your little Prada suit and bloody nose out of this office before I call security."

"I'm the one that's going to call security, you asshole. Do you know who I am?" Jacob snarled.

Seriously? That's what he went with. I could have laughed at the farce, but with the blood in August's eyes, and the temper in Jacob's, I moved between them, my hands shaking for an instant before I forced myself to steady.

"Stop it. Both of you. Just go, Jacob. We have nothing to discuss. And if you dare sue or threaten August in any way, remember, Jacob, there are reasons you want me to sign a non-disclosure." I narrowed my gaze at him, as he just glowered. "I know things, Jacob. You want to be powerful? You want the next step in your career that you feel like you were owed?

Remember that you are not an innocent party here. If you touch him in any way, I will make it worse for you. I don't need to lay a hand on you to do it."

"This isn't over," Jacob growled, but he turned on his heel anyway, leaving me alone in the office with August.

It had been so stupid to threaten Jacob. Because I could be all talk in that instance, but Jacob could hurt me a lot more than I could hurt him in some ways. Because he had his family, and I only had my dear old mother.

"What the hell, Paisley? How dare you put yourself in the middle of that, where you could have gotten hurt!"

I spun on him, mouth gaping. "I cannot believe you just did that."

My ex-husband just stared at me, confusion etched on his face, and I had to wonder why anyone kept coming here—they were always either threatening me or trying to protect me.

I had been doing just fine on my own for so long, I didn't need them now.

And yet here August was, my memory, my past, and a man that would never be my future.

And all I wanted to do was scream.

Chapter Eleven

August

P aisley whirled on me. "I cannot believe you just did that."

I frowned, wondering what the hell she could possibly mean. It wasn't as if I had kicked the guy in the nuts or gutted him like I had wanted to. Jacob would've earned those outcomes considering he had dared put his hands on her.

"What do you mean?"

"You know exactly what I mean. You can't just beat up anybody who stands in your way."

I took a step back, shaking my head. "That's what you think that was? That I just had a little disagreement with that asshole and suddenly what, I can't handle myself? Get a fucking clue, Paisley. He put his hands on you."

"He didn't." She ran her hands over her face, looking as exhausted as I felt in that moment. "Okay, he touched me, but I was fine. I was *fine*. He was hovering over me, but I was handling it. I've always been able to handle him."

Sheer rage slid over me. "Are you fucking kidding me? How many times has he done this to you? You told me he didn't hurt you that way. Were you lying about him? Because I will go out there right now and kill him. He doesn't get to touch you."

"And you don't get to try to protect me from him. I can do that myself."

"Yes. Because you could always do everything by yourself, Paisley Cassidy Renee."

"Don't full name me. You have no right to stand in here and yell at me and try to take over. We were both very clear that we have nothing to do with each other than our shared connections."

"And yet, what were you going to do to Jacob to get him out of your office? Where's your fucking security? Why are you here alone where anybody can just come in?"

"My security is on a different floor at the moment as they're closing up. I was just packing my things so I could go home."

"And yet he was allowed to come up here."

"Because he was my husband. And apparently whoever's at the front desk decided that he was allowed to be up here. Do not worry, I will take care of that."

"Yes, because you'll *take care of that*."

"Don't say that so sarcastically. I can handle things on my own."

"Didn't look like that from here."

"Fuck you."

"Yes, so original."

"You're the one who tried to use his fists. So I don't know what you're talking about being original here."

"They let me up here without a second thought because I'm apparently family."

She blanched. "What?"

"Yes, because I'm family with two of the women that work here, and they know that I'm your ex-husband, so they just let me up here. What kind of fucking shit show for security are you running here?"

"Apparently one that I need to change," she said, letting out a breath. "He didn't hurt me, August."

"Why don't I believe you?"

"I'm fine. He's not here anymore. And he's not coming back."

Underneath the bravado, finally I could see the fear. Not of me, hopefully never of me. But of that man.

I let out a breath, my heart rate finally being able to

slow down. Because that first tableau I had witnessed when I had walked into this office? It had nearly taken ten years off my life. Jacob had hovered over her, caging her within his arms against the desk. And there had been nothing I could do until I was suddenly on his back, pulling the man away. If I had been just seconds later, what would that man have done to her? It didn't bear even thinking about, and yet I knew those would be the only thoughts running through my mind for far too long. The only thing that ever echoed in my memories. The look of her fear right then and there, and the fact that she had looked so helpless in front of her ex-husband. And Paisley never looked helpless. Even when she looked as if she were falling underneath the weight of a thousand commands and responsibilities, she never looked as if she couldn't handle it. And yet clearly, something had happened.

"Why was he here? And what did you threaten him with?"

She took a step away then and headed over to the beverage cabinet. I thought she would pour whiskey or something else absurd that businesspeople always seem to do in the movies, but instead, she poured two glasses of water in lowball glasses, and handed me one. I took it, and frowned, before she downed half of hers in one gulp.

Well, she was far more rattled than I thought.

"Paisley." When she didn't say anything, a cold sensation spread through my chest. "Paisley. What happened with pretty boy?"

Her eyes flashed for a moment, exactly what I had wanted. I didn't care about the fuck face, Jacob. But I did care about what he was doing to her. I would have to dig a little deeper about what all that meant later. But for now, I needed to know.

"He wanted to make sure I was going to sign an extra non-disclosure. Evidently he doesn't want any of his dirty secrets out in the world. Even though I already told him I wouldn't be signing it, and there was nothing he could do about it. It wasn't part of our prenups, and he can't make me." She held up her hand before I could say anything. "Not that I would have said anything to begin with. I just want to be out of the news. I want people to see what we're doing here at work. See the good, the money we're raising to help others. I want them to see women in business kicking ass. I don't want to be the bitter ex-wife. But I'll absolutely play that part if he comes after you. If he threatens to sue you, I will go to the press, I will tell them everything I know about him. All about his cheating, and any business ties that might be a little shady. I will tell them everything."

I cursed under my breath and moved forward after

setting the water glass down. "You don't have to protect me, Paisley."

"I think I just said the same to you."

I cursed under my breath, and moved forward, not realizing my hand was already outstretched, my fingers gently grazing her cheek. She stiffened for a moment, before swallowing hard.

"Paise..."

"What are you doing here?" she asked, bringing me back to the present.

"I am just glad you're okay."

"I've forever been fine, August. Jacob can't hurt me anymore."

I thought I heard the lie in her voice, but instead I just continued to hold her cheek, cradling her as she stared up at me, both of us not speaking.

I kept thinking about what could have happened. What Jacob had been thinking in that moment. Because while I knew Paisley could handle anything, that man was so much bigger than her. And I wish I could find him and finish the job. But that wouldn't accomplish anything, I knew that.

Jacob held so much more power than I ever could, but I was just the low life who could try to take that power back.

"What are you doing here, August?" Paisley asked again after a moment, bringing me out of my thoughts.

I blinked, swallowing hard. "I just...I thought we should talk."

Such a lame thing to say after everything that had happened. But I had come here to talk to her. I didn't know what about. Only I hadn't been able to stop thinking about her all day at work.

I had been teaching students about chemical bonds and reactions, all the while having Paisley's voice in my head, telling me to keep going, or that it wasn't enough. And it didn't always have to do with what had happened in that suite. I hadn't even realized that I was driving toward her building until I was already parking, knowing that I needed to see her.

This was the exact opposite of what I had told myself I would be doing. I did not need to be near her. I needed to take a step back and not want this. But I was still touching her, still looking into those eyes of hers that had drawn me in. She was my addiction, my drug of choice, and I knew I needed to quit her long ago. Just like I had before.

And then I wasn't moving.

"We were so good at talking before, right?" Paisley asked, rolling her eyes. But she didn't move away.

Instead we stood there, her office door closed, the

two of us alone, and I couldn't help but make wrong choice after wrong choice.

I leaned down and brushed my lips against hers, needing to know she was safe, that she was real.

Her lips parted in surprise, but she didn't pull away, instead she leaned forward, going on her tiptoes, and kissing me back.

"Paisley. He could have hurt you."

"But he didn't," she whispered against my lips.

And so I deepened the kiss, sliding my hand around to the back of her neck, holding her steady as my tongue slid against hers.

She moaned, and I moaned right back, her hands sliding down my sides to grip the belt loops of my jeans.

I let my other hand fall to her waist, squeezing gently, needing her touch, just needing her.

I would think about the consequences of what that thought meant later. I was so good about pretending that I would, but it didn't matter in that moment.

Instead I continued to kiss her, sliding my lips along her jaw and then down her neck.

"Tell me to go. And I'll go."

But I wouldn't want to.

But she didn't, instead she pulled at my belt loops, tugging me toward her, and I let her.

She tasted of sweetness, and Paisley, and I

continued to lap at her, needing every inch of her. I pulled away slightly, ignoring the frown on her face at the movement, before adjusting us both so we were at her desk. And then I was pulling off her shirt, one button at a time, and she was tugging at my Henley. I undid the blouse, the silk falling to the floor, and she stood there in a discreet bra that showed off the top half of her tits and lifted them up, and a business skirt with a slit up the side.

I groaned, gently running my hands up that slit.

"What kind of panties are you wearing?" I growled into her ear.

"Why don't you find out?"

I bit gently down on her ear, and she tilted her head back. I couldn't walk away from the invitation, so I licked up her neck, before biting gently down again.

She moaned, arching into me. I slid my hand around her backside, her soft skin bare under my palm. So when my fingers brushed against the edge of her thong, I slid it to the side, easing my fingers in between her ass cheeks.

"A thong? You don't like panty lines, do you?"

"I hate them. But I don't know if I like the breeze if I go pantiless."

"One day you'll go pantiless for me. So that way I know that just a bare touch and I'll be between your legs. Would you do that?"

"August," she whispered.

"I love the sound of my name on your lips."

My hands in between her legs, she arched into me, and I played with her hole, just pressing against the pucker, loving the way that she moaned. And then I continued my exploration, one finger and then the second down to her pussy.

"Already so wet for me. You're drenching that thong, aren't you?"

"I can't help it," she gasped.

"Let me take care of that for you."

So she leaned forward, her breasts against my chest as she gripped my arms, her back arched in an invitation. I slid one finger inside her heat, her cunt clamping around my finger.

"You're soaked."

And then I inserted another, before gently teasing, one sliding in and then out, then along her seam, then back to that puckered hole.

"Are you going to let me fuck your ass like before? Do you want my cock inside you, stretching you?"

"August, I can't take any more."

"Yes, you can." And then I slid one finger deep inside her, using her own juices to help the penetration. And she moaned, shaking.

"That's it, that's my girl."

But at this angle, I wouldn't be able to see every-thing, so I slid my fingers out, ignoring her moan, then twisted her so her front was to me.

"Let me see your tits. Take off that bra."

"Are you serious right now?"

"Do it."

She undid the clasp on the bra, her breasts falling heavy in front of me. I reached out and pinched one nipple, loving the way that her mouth parted. And then I took her by the hips and turned her so that her back faced me.

"Bend over, I wasn't finished."

"So bossy."

I squeezed her other breast, just gently, loving the way that her eyes darkened as she looked over her shoulder.

"You like it."

She didn't say anything, but then she let me turn her fully, her hands on the desk, and then I was pulling her skirt up so I could see that luscious ass of hers.

I tugged the thong to the side and speared her with two fingers without warning. She gasped, her back arching again, and I finger-fucked her, loving the way the sounds of sex filled the room. Then I used her juices to continue to pleasure her as much as I could, using my middle finger in her pussy, my thumb playing with her puckered hole. She shook, her knees nearly going weak, but I kept her steady, until I knelt down in front of her, and licked up her cunt.

She came right then and there, the tip of my tongue playing with her clit, as she gushed over my face, and I continued to lick and suck at her. When I removed my fingers, she bent over the desk, her legs going weak, but I kept her steady. Because I would never let anyone hurt her.

No, I would just be the one who did that. I pushed that thought from my mind, before I squeezed her ass, continuing to massage her.

"You're so fucking beautiful."

"August. I can't."

"You will."

I pulled off her skirt, but I kept her heels on. The sight of her naked in stilettos was the most beautiful thing I had ever seen.

And then she stood up and turned, and I gently massaged her breasts, keeping my gaze on her.

"Do you want to come again?"

"From the look of that tent pole straining in your jeans right now, I think it's my turn."

I grinned, then took my hands to her shoulders and gently pushed her down to her knees.

"Do you need something to protect your skin?" I asked.

She shook her head as she undid my belt buckle.

"No, the carpet's soft."

"That's a good girl," I whispered, putting her hair into a ponytail as she gripped the base of my cock, pulling the length of me out of my boxer shorts.

"Suck it, let me fuck your mouth."

"This is my office—shouldn't I be the boss here?"

I tugged on her hair, forcing her gaze to mine.

"Not right now."

She nodded, before she licked the tip of my cock, and I groaned.

When she swallowed me whole, hollowing her cheeks and humming along my cock so it touched the back of her throat, I nearly came right then.

With one hand on my balls, massaging them in her palm, she used the other hand to grip the base of my cock since not all of it could fit in her mouth. She bobbed her head, with me guiding the motion, the back of my spine tingling with the exertion of me holding back. But I needed to be inside her. I didn't want to come down her throat or over those pretty breasts like I had in the past. No, I needed to be inside that pussy of hers. Even if I knew it was a mistake.

And when I almost came, I pulled back, and then tugged her to her feet so I could crush my mouth to hers.

"You're way too good at that."

"I'm glad you think so," she said with a wink, and then I was picking her up by her waist and sitting her on her desk.

"This is most unhygienic for my office."

"Sue me. We'll clean up later."

And then I crushed my mouth to hers before I pulled away and pushed her back so she lay over her desk, pushing the keyboard away, knocking a few things on the floor.

She let out a little giggle that made me smile, and so I pulled at her thighs, so her ass was right at the edge of the desk.

"Ready?"

For an instant she met my gaze, and I was afraid she was going to say no. Then again, I didn't know if I was ready for this either.

But instead she nodded, playing with her own breasts, and so I plunged into her in one thrust, her pussy so tight around my cock I nearly came.

She shouted my name, and I continued to move, wrapping one of her legs around my waist and pulling her other leg so that her ankle was on my shoulder. I pounded into her, loving the way that her breasts bounced when she had to remove her hands to keep herself steady on the desk.

When I slid one leg between her legs, letting her rest her other leg on my shoulder, I slid my thumb over her clit, and she came, one touch, and she was gone, clamping down on me so tight that I nearly saw stars. So I came with her, lowering her leg so I could lean over her to take her mouth. I kept moving, even through the orgasm, as I helped her to a sitting position. She wrapped both legs around me, arching for me thrust for thrust, as I continued to kiss her, needing her touch.

I knew we would have to talk about this. We would have to deal.

Not now. Instead, after the orgasms faded, and we came down from our high, we just held each other, locked together, physically, emotionally, and with every memory in between.

Then I just held her and felt the tears against my chest.

And I knew some were for me, but not all. The only thing I could do was hold her. I wasn't sure what else I could do.

"He won't come back," I promised. "He won't."

"I know," she whispered against me, this time running her hands down my back as if in comfort.

And I knew I had fallen. Once again. And there was no going back.

Even if there was no future in what we had just done.

Chapter Twelve

Paisley

I set out the last plate and hoped my house was as childproof as possible. The girls didn't bring Hayleigh and Keelie over often, mostly because it was easier for me to just go over to their places since I didn't have a children's room with all the toys and cribs, but I had slowly begun to add things so that way the girls and whatever future children my friends had would be comfortable at my place. I had a travel crib, and a few toys and learning enrichment activities. It wasn't much, and it wasn't enough, but I was doing my best to add more. I wanted my friends and their children to be comfortable here, because markedly, I was going to be the cool aunt. I wanted to be that cool aunt. The one that those little girls could come to if they needed help in which they couldn't ask their parents for. Not that I thought that that would ever be the case when it came to my friend group. It wasn't like our parents' were. There was that disconnect and feeling of hurt and near-hatred.

I just wanted to be somebody that people trusted to come to if they needed something.

Which was highly hypocritical of me considering I hadn't told my best friends about the divorce, nor the fact that I had slept with August. Not once. But twice.

It wasn't like August and I were talking about it. Even though he had come to the office to talk, we hadn't. Instead we had fallen together again, and now were acting like nothing had happened.

Except it had, and we needed to discuss it. In depth, and annoyingly so. Only I wasn't sure what I wanted to say.

Because I loved him. I wanted him. And I knew I couldn't have him.

Because he hadn't wanted me all those years ago, so I needed to take care of myself.

Only I didn't think that was really what was going to happen.

The doorbell rang, and I was saved from my own wandering thoughts. I smoothed out my shirt, and snorted at myself considering that these were my best friends who would see me at my worst. It didn't matter what I was wearing.

When I opened the door, Hayleigh and Keelie ran toward me, arms outstretched.

"My babies!" I called out, as I fell to my knees, and held them close. They started rambling at what felt like a thousand words a minute, and I rained kisses all over their faces, and tickled their tummies, and fell in love with my honorary nieces all over again.

"You two are growing so fast. Are you all ready for college?"

"Don't joke about things like that, I'm not ready." Addison winked as she said it, walking in past us with Devney on her heels. They held bags of food and drinks, even though I had enough for everyone. But that's what we did. We took care of each other.

This was a good reminder of that.

As the girls' voices filled the room, I closed the door behind them, standing up so I could hold both of their hands. We walked into the living room, and I answered their questions, yes, I loved their outfits, no I hadn't seen a unicorn that day but I was going to keep a lookout, and yes, I did have my tiara in the shop, but I would show them soon.

Considering I had been on the pageant circuit when I was younger thanks to my overbearing mother, I had tiaras for them to look at. I had a couple that I would wait until they were a little bit older so that they could play with.

I couldn't quite believe I had kept them all, but it had been a part of my life, and I couldn't throw things away. Hence why I still had that memory box of me and August's things.

I pushed him from my mind for just a moment because I needed to focus on the here and now. And let my friends know what was happening. Just not with the little girls around.

"We come bearing gifts," Devney said, as she leaned forward and kissed my cheek. "And cheese."

"You and your cheese addiction," I said.

"What? I like cheese."

"And I like cured meats. It's like we're a match made in heaven."

"Well, don't worry, I have crackers, and a bunch of dried fruit and dips and nuts to make our own boards."

"This sounds fun to me," Addison said. Then she studied my face. "Are you going to talk about what's been bothering you?"

I nodded, knowing they needed to know everything. About Jacob, my mother, and August. I was probably going need a lot of wine for today.

"Yes. But maybe without little ears," I whispered, as

the girls played in the living room behind us, both laughing and looking carefree.

Addison's eyes widened, and I realized she had been expecting me to turn away from the problem. After all, that's what I was good at. I was going to do better.

I had to do better.

"Okay, this sounds like it was a good idea that I brought the sparkling wine," Devney said, her voice oddly cheerful. "I'm going to stick that in the fridge, so it's ready for us after lunch and before N-A-P time, and then we're good to go."

"What happens when they learn to spell?" I asked, honestly curious.

"Then we whisper and make up other words," Addison said with a shrug. "Honestly, I just do what the baby books say, and then wing it. Luca's better at this than me most of the time."

"Heath too. It's a little disconcerting how good he is at it."

"They're great dads. You're lucky."

"Considering what they grew up with? Honestly, I'm surprised at what great parents they are."

"I guess it goes to show you it's not who raised you, but who you've become on your own."

At least I hoped that was true as well. I'd thought I'd be a mom by now, looking forward to the next phases of my life as I figured out the trials and tribulations of motherhood and happiness.

My father had been decent. At least in some aspects. But he was long gone, and I had been left with my mother. The woman who had pushed me into becoming a beauty queen, not even for a scholarship, just so she could lord it over everyone else that I was Miss Little Portland, or Miss Strawberry Fields. Then I had to be the best at spelling bee. I had to win not just my school, not just the district, but I had to win the state. And when I had gotten second place, it was the first time my mother had truly hit me. And then I kept going. I had run track, done swim team. I had been the cheerleader, and the prom queen. But I had only made prom queen my senior year; my junior year I hadn't even made the court. And so my mother had punished me for that. I had been forced to have the perfect boyfriends in high school, the ones with the chiseled jaws even though we were teenagers, and the ones with the most connections with their parents. I hadn't even realized she had been setting me up on those so-called play dates when I had been in middle school, not realizing that she was trying to plan my entire life.

So my defiance had been August.

A boy who had made me smile in college and I had fallen in love with. The man I had married and thought

I would spend the rest of my life with. I knew I was going to take over my own world and soar in my business because I had no other option. And not just because my mother had wanted it that way. But because I was damn good at it. And I had loved August's mind. He was brilliant, an amazing scientist, and he had known he had wanted to go into teaching. He had wanted to make sure that he emulated teachers who had helped him thrive.

And knowing how he had grown up, how his parents had such a tumultuous relationship with him and had taken away his base, it only made sense that he would've wanted something steady.

And I was all in with that. It didn't matter that he didn't want to pursue research or academia with all the highlights and accomplishments that could come from that. I didn't care that sometimes he had to teach driver's ed in order to pay the bills because teachers were never paid enough in this country. In my mind, I could make enough for both of us, so that way we could both do what we wanted. And I hadn't thought August cared about that. I just thought he loved me for me.

But he had walked away, and now somehow, he was back. Because what, we couldn't stand to be away from each other? Because he wanted my body but not my heart or my future?

I shook my head at myself even as I listened halfheartedly to Addison and Devney talk about the upcoming wedding.

It was odd to think that so much had changed and yet nothing had changed. I was sitting in a room with my two best friends and their children, and I was alone.

And yet I had this secret. I still had the slight bruises on my body from August, but they were the bruises that came from need and desire and want. They were consensual.

And I hadn't told anyone about them. I hated secrets.

"They're planning this big elaborate thing, and I cannot believe it. It's their third wedding," Devney mumbled, as she poured a glass of wine.

The children were now tucked in the guest room, old enough for my guest bed and cuddled together for their nap.

They had looked so cute when we had tucked them in, and now it was adult time with our own conversations where we didn't have to spell out certain things.

"So they're really going through with it? They're marrying each other again?" I asked, still aghast.

"Yep. Apparently third time's the charm."

I winced at that. "Well, I can't really say much about that because if I ever get married again, which as far as I'm concerned is a big no, it will be my third time."

Addison paled, before she reached out and gripped my hand. "I did not mean it like that. I meant third time with each other. You have a very different set of circumstances."

I shook my head. "I don't know if it feels that different. Considering it's a lot of the same players."

"No. We're going to get into everything about you in a second, but those two?" Devney shook her head. "Their version of love is not something that I ever want in our lives. They do it for the drama, and the flair. And they're forcing their kids to be part of this because somehow, they convinced them that this was going to work. If it was up to me, I would walk away and never look back."

My eyes widened at her harsh statement. Devney was the sweetest among us. She had a huge family, with multiple siblings that were all either getting married, were already married, or along the way. Her blended family was loud, chaotic, and ridiculously happy.

Even with the torment in their past, they were happy.

And Devney was the selfless one. There was caring and understanding. And yet, she'd held firm against Heath's parents.

"So you're all going to this."

"Yes, because Heath and his siblings have all stated

that this will be the last one. That they are done placating them."

"And Luca's right along with them. They're going to go, watch it happen, and then hope for the best. Because we're going to protect our kids no matter what."

"You guys are good parents."

"We're trying. Now, tell us what's wrong," Addison whispered.

I swallowed hard, then reached for my wine glass.

"I've slept with August. Twice."

I hadn't meant to blurt it out just then. I had been wanting to lead up to it, to find a common ground and perhaps eloquently state it. But no, of course I hadn't.

Devney and Addison looked at each other and then at me.

"You mean besides the time at the resort?" Devney asked.

Addison nodded. "What she said."

I choked on my wine before setting it down quickly so I could take a napkin and wipe the splatter down my shirt.

"Are you serious right now? You knew this whole time?"

"Of course we knew you slept with him. You couldn't have hidden it. We thought maybe it was just a one-night thing because of proximity? Are there feelings? We just don't know these things. But oh my God. Paisley. Twice?"

Devney sounded aghast, and frankly I felt the same way too.

"Yes, twice."

I explained about the resort, and how it had just accidentally happened after we had been fighting, and both girls fanned themselves even as I rolled my eyes.

"You don't think this is weird? Considering that he's your brother-in-law, and literally your husband's twin," I pointed at Devney.

"Well, they're identical, so I can tell you that you probably had a good time," she said, before she blushed hard and gulped her wine.

Addison threw her head back and laughed, and I just lifted my glass in a toast.

"Well, there is that. Because my God. That man. He was like that. Even when we were younger, but I think he just got better. Which makes me think he had practice, and then I want to throw up."

"Well, practice helps, because you had practice." Addison winced. "I'm not saying the right thing now."

"No, it's fine. We had lives. We moved on. And then Jacob showed up at my office."

Addison leaned forward. "What? Wait. Whoa. Back up. Your ex showed up?"

I let out a breath. "After my mother left and you left, Jacob showed up."

"It all happened that day!" Devney exclaimed.

"Yep. It was an eventful day. And I sort of broke my computer."

Both girls looked at each other, then at me.

"Go into detail. *Very, very* explicit detail," Addison blurted, and I laughed.

"Jacob showed up and got growly because he wants me to sign non-disclosure papers. It doesn't matter because most of it wouldn't even be legally binding anyway. But he got rude, and then well he sort of cornered me."

"That asshole. I'm going to kill him."

I shook my head at Addison's words, even though Devney stood up, ready to punch out a man who wasn't even in the room.

"It's fine. Because then August showed up, and I think he might've broken Jacob's nose."

"I love that man," Addison said, as she stood up, and lifted her fists into the air. "See? The Cassidy brothers will drive you insane, but they are good men."

"Well, and then I had to threaten Jacob because he was probably going to sue August, and it was a whole thing. I got Jacob out of the office, and that left me and August alone."

"And? Go into detail," Devney urged.

My lips twitched. This felt so normal, and something that we had been neglecting for far too long.

"And then he said he wanted to talk, and we didn't talk. Instead we had sex, a lot of sex. Dirty sex. All over my desk."

"Oh my God. And we just showed up in your office the next day, when there was like sex all over the furniture?" Addison asked, before she downed the rest of her wine.

"Well, we cleaned it. As much as possible. But my computer broke. And it's a whole thing. However, we didn't talk. So God forbid we know what's going on."

"I don't even want to go into what a label could be with this, but you didn't talk at all?"

"No. He divorced me. He's the one who walked away all those years ago. And then he puts his hand on the back of my neck and tells me to kiss him or to be a good girl, and then I can't help myself."

I put my hand over my mouth, as both women hooted in laughter before quieting down so they wouldn't wake the children.

"I didn't mean to get that much into detail."

"Oh no, please do," Addison said with a grin.

"Either way, I feel like I'm lost here. He didn't love me enough to stay, and now we can't even be adults and talk about what we're feeling. We just keep falling into each other, and we're in each other's orbits because I'm friends with you guys, and I don't know, it's complicated."

"What do you want to happen?" Devney asked.

I shook my head. "That's the problem. I don't know. Because I think I love him. I think I've always loved him. And I married another man even though I loved August. What kind of person does that make me?"

"A person that needs to talk with August," Addison said softly, and I sighed, knowing they were right.

So I sank back into my chair as we turned to water and changed the subject.

Because I wasn't going to get any answers today, not without talking to the man in question.

Only I was truly afraid of the answers.

If he even deigned to give me one.

Chapter Thirteen

August

As I sat down on the weight bench, weight in hand, I stared at my brothers.

We had all come over to Luca's house to work out, but then we had gotten distracted by a golden retriever who Luca was taking care of for the evening, and the fact that the golden retriever didn't quite like Luca's cat. But now the two were becoming fast friends, and we were late on our workouts. Their wives and children were over at Paisley's house for a girls' evening, so we guys were just hanging out, while Greer was over with her husbands.

It was nice, having this time together, even though I was still a little confused as to what the hell I was supposed to be doing with my life.

I hadn't planned on this. I hadn't planned on any of

this. But now I needed to figure out what I was going to do with Paisley.

"You have your thinking face on, and it honestly looks a little painful."

I flipped Heath off. "Fuck you."

"No, thanks. Seriously though, that thinking face looks like it hurts."

"I have the same damn face as you. I don't know why you think you're funny."

"Because I'm freaking hilarious."

Luca just shook his head at us.

"So, why the thinking face? Hard chemistry problem? Like what happens to oxygen once it leaves hydrogen peroxide?" Luca asked, and I snorted.

"I can tell you the answer if you want."

"I want to know," Heath asked, and Luca snorted.

"You should know the answer. I know the answer."

"Because you are the wunderkind who is a veterinarian and should know the answer." I winked at him, then glared over at Heath. "Hydrogen peroxide is just H_2O_2. It literally has this little oxygen-oxygen single bond and then once it hits light, it decomposes and you have water and O_2. Get it? H_2O and O_2?"

"Really? That's it."

"Yes. Basic chemistry can be fun."

"I'm literally yawning deep inside. I cannot believe you just said that."

"I'm just saying, it's why they come in the little dark bottles."

"You're ridiculous. And now that we've had our chemistry lesson for the day, please, enlighten me on why you had that annoying face on."

"Again, it's your face," I growled. I did another rep and sighed. "I slept with Paisley."

"We know that. We *heard* that," Luca said with an obvious shudder.

"No. We slept together again." I paused as they both stared at me wide-eyed. "In her office. On her desk. We might have broken a lamp. I'm not sure. But yeah, we had sex. Twice. In her office. And I don't think there's enough Clorox to take away everything."

"My wife works in that office," Heath snapped.

"So does mine," Luca put in.

"Seriously?" both said at the same time, and I set down the weight before pinching the bridge of my nose.

"I realize that we shouldn't have. I realize it was very inappropriate, but it just happened."

"You just fell into her vagina?" Heath asked, and Luca let out a groan.

"Really? That's what you're going to say?"

"What else am I supposed to say? When he says that

he sleeps with his ex-wife, not once, but a second time and says it's an accident? I worry about this man."

"The first kiss was an accident, and I told myself it was a mistake, and then I kept going. I like having sex with Paisley. That was never our problem. She has forever been the best thing I've ever had."

However I knew as I said that, I wasn't talking about sex in that instant. Because she had been the best thing I had ever had. And I had walked away from it.

"What the hell had you been thinking when you left her?" Heath asked softly.

"I want to say I hadn't been thinking, but I thought too much all those years ago."

"What happened all those years ago, man?" Heath asked, as both of my brothers set down the workout equipment to stare at me.

"It wasn't the right time for us."

"Bullshit," Luca burst out, surprising all of us, considering Luca was the calm one of us.

"Bullshit," Luca repeated. "I remember the way you two were. Yes, you fought, but in that playful way that you two sometimes do now. You two were fucking amazing together. And then suddenly you're finishing up college and you're ready to start your new phases, and you're alone, and she isn't coming by anymore. It's just over and you're not telling us what happened. Did you fucking cheat on her? Did she cheat on you?"

I didn't even realize I was in Luca's face before Heath was pulling us apart.

"Don't you ever fucking say that again. I would have never touched another woman."

"Then what happened?"

"She didn't cheat on me. It wasn't anything like that. I walked away because I had to."

"Why? What was so important that you couldn't be with the woman that made you happy? Then again, I don't even know why our parents can never seem to love each other. So at the time, I figured it was just something our family did. But I see the way that I'm with Addison, and Heath is with Devney. And the way that you look at Paisley when she's not looking. What the hell, August?"

I glared at my brother, trying to suck in breath, before I looked over at Heath who just waved at me.

"Well? Talk to us. What happened?"

"Have you seen Paisley?" I burst out.

"What?" Luca snapped.

"Have you seen her? And not just how beautiful she is, because she's the most absolute beautiful woman I've ever met in my life. But she's caring, and yet prideful. She raises her chin when she's scared and she's trying to hide it. And she is brilliant. She is a multimillionaire who is poised to take over the world. She was always good with money, and might have come from some of it, but what she has now? It makes everything else pale in comparison. She had everything going for her, and she was married to a future *high school chemistry teacher*." I didn't mean to put such anger in the title, but there it was, out, and there was nothing else I could do.

"You've got to be fucking kidding me," Heath growled. "Don't tell me you broke up with her for her own good. Because I'm going to beat the shit out of you for even saying it."

"She kept canceling things to stay with me. Because I only had certain weekends off during my internship. She was afraid to travel without me because my schedule didn't work. It wasn't like I could take PTO in order to go with her to some of these conferences. So she was alone so much, even when she was working even more hours than me, our schedules didn't mesh, our lives didn't mesh. She was exceptionalism personified, and I was the guy with a family who couldn't stay together, and a job that I loved, but didn't fit with hers."

My heart raced as I said the words, even as I realized that it didn't make any sense. And yet, there were more reasons. More reasons that made bile rise in my throat.

"You dumped her because she was too successful?" Luca asked, each word a staccato beat.

"I walked away so she could bloom. So she could thrive. And if I hadn't, her mother—" I cut myself off before I could say anything else, and then Heath was in my face, Luca right beside him.

"What the hell did that bitch do?" Heath asked, his voice low.

Well, it seemed that Heath remembered Paisley's mother from the wedding, or perhaps had met her along the way with Devney's job.

"Her mother had plans for Paisley."

"And you just let it happen? Her mom had plans with Paisley's ex-husband as well, and we see how that turned out."

"It wasn't just that. There was a big deal at the start of Paisley's company that she needed to focus on, and her mother wanted that deal to happen more than anything but swore to me if I held her daughter back..." My voice trailed off as I swallowed that bile once again, my hands shaking.

"What did her mother say she'd do? That she'd ruin the deal? The deal that she wanted her daughter to have?" Luca asked. "I don't buy it."

"Her mother tried to sell her to the highest bidder right out of college," I growled. "It didn't matter that we were engaged at the time. She kept introducing her to these older men who wanted younger wives with money. The same way that she sold off Paisley in the beauty circuit, and all through school with all those championships that she won. Paisley always had to be perfect. And I was the stain on that perfection."

"But not in Paisley's eyes. In her mother's. What the hell were you thinking?"

"If I had stayed, Paisley would have lost everything. She would have lost the business. She would have lost the proposal she needed that's launched her into the success she is now. I don't know what the plan was after I left, but that was what was going to happen. Paisley was going to lose everything if I stayed. And she wouldn't have been able to grow with me. So I left. It was the best thing I could do for her."

"You're lucky I don't beat the shit out of you right now," Heath whispered, before he stepped away, shaking his head.

"And Paisley has no idea this happened."

"No. I just filed for divorce and walked away. But look at her now. Look at everything she's done. She keeps your wives employed."

"Fuck that. They would have found other companies where they had other jobs. And even then, Paisley could have built something else from the ground up. Have you seen that woman work? She is a fucking savant at this shit," Luca said. "And you took that choice away from her. For her to fight for herself. Instead you had to be the sacrificial knight."

"Her mother is already trying to sell her off to Jacob again, so I don't know what would have happened back then. All I know is if I had stayed, she would have lost everything. And she wouldn't have been able to grow."

"It sounds to me you were embarrassed about our family. And hell, I was embarrassed too." Heath let out a breath. "Embarrassed about our parents. About the fact that we didn't even know our baby sister. So yeah, I get that. But you are an amazing teacher. You need to remember that. Hell, you still teach me things every day. And we're fucking twins. I thought we were supposed to have twin minds and all that," Heath said, scoffing at his poor execution of a joke.

"I did what I thought was best at the time. I don't even think my frontal lobe was fully developed."

"Are we sure it is now?" Luca asked, concern in his gaze. "What are you going to do about this? You need to tell her."

I shook my head. "If I tell her, she'll hate me."

"I'm pretty sure she already hated you for leaving in the first place," Heath put in.

"But what good would it do if I told her? I'm not going to be our parents. I'm not going to marry the same woman again."

"How the hell does that make you our parents? Other than the actual causality here. It's just a comparison. And I'm not saying that you should marry her, but maybe you should have a damn conversation," Luca snapped.

"If I tell her, it will hurt her. And I've already done that enough."

"Keeping her in the dark is hurting her too. And I cannot believe I'm the one having this conversation because you know I hate talking about my fucking feelings," Heath roared.

My lips twitched despite the subject, and I sighed.

"I don't know what's going to happen between Paisley and me. Because if we do something, and it falls apart, she's not going to have anyone. You're her family."

"Then figure it out so no one gets hurt," Luca said simply even though there was nothing simple about it. "Because you deserve happiness too."

I sighed, before I picked up my water bottle and walked toward the door.

"I'm going to make my way home. Don't feel like finishing working out."

"Think about it. Talk to her. She deserves to know." I nodded at Heath's words, then headed out to my car.

I knew that the guys wouldn't tell Paisley, but they

might tell their wives. And they should. Because there shouldn't be secrets.

And how rich was that coming from me.

I got on the highway, but instead of taking my exit, I took hers. I wasn't quite sure what I was supposed to say to her, or even if it would be tonight. But maybe I would figure out something.

So when I found myself in front of her door, the driveway empty, telling me that the girls had left, I let out a breath, and was grateful when she opened the door.

She had a glass of wine in her hand, with just leggings on, and her sports bra.

I raised a brow. "You're working out?"

"I was going to get into some yoga with some wine after the girls left. I'm all edgy. What's wrong, August?" she asked as she took a step back. I moved inside and noticed that she had on hot-pink toenail polish.

Why the hell was that sexy?

"Come with me to the wedding," I blurted. I hadn't even realized I was going to say the words at all. But they were out there now, and I wanted to say them.

She stared at me, then gestured with the wine glass toward the rest of the bottle on the counter.

"Do you want to pour yourself a glass of wine and repeat that?"

I laughed, then sighed and walked to the counter, and did indeed pour myself a glass. "Come with me to the wedding. I feel like I'm going to punch someone when I'm there."

"And you want to take me with you for that?" she said dryly.

My eyes widened and I turned to her. "No. I want someone I know that's going to be there." I winced. "I want you there, Paisley. And I don't know what this means, and I know we should talk about it, but hell, you should be there for the show."

She sighed, then pulled on my shirt so I moved forward.

"Okay."

"Yeah?"

"Okay. I want to see the show."

I leaned down and brushed my lips against hers. "Thank you, Paise."

"No problem, Augie."

"You know I hate that name."

"True. Do you want to stay?" she asked, her voice soft, and my shoulders relaxed. I hadn't even realized I had been tense since I had walked out of that office.

"Yeah?"

It was a question, not a statement, and she smiled.

"Yeah. Stay the night. And then I'll go with you to that wedding. And I'll look fabulous."

"I think that won't be too difficult."

"Look at you, with all the compliments."

"I try."

She studied my face, and I knew there were questions there, with answers that I was afraid to give.

But she didn't ask them, and I didn't ask her anything either. Instead, I let her drag me down the hall, and I went easily.

Greedily.

I didn't know when I would tell her the truth. Or what good it would do.

All I knew was that I wanted to be with her tonight.

And she had asked me to stay.

Chapter Fourteen

Paisley

There were only so many times I could look at myself in the mirror and call my choices a mistake before I realized I had to own up to them. Which probably wasn't the best way to start my morning, but honestly, I wasn't sure what else there was to do.

I'd gone and fallen back in love with my ex-husband and there was no denying what was happening. Even if this whole thing exploded and there was nothing left for us but the remains of who we'd once been, I'd still have these feelings.

And the honest part of myself that was getting harder to ignore as time moved on knew that I'd always been in love with him. Because there were *reasons* why I felt as if part of me broke day by day as I tried to catch up with who I had once been. I had been looking for August in all the interactions I had with others without realizing it.

I'd married the wrong man because I'd thought I'd needed that love.

And I'd married the right man at the wrong time because I'd thought that love was all I'd needed.

And as I sat here in front of the vanity mirror in the hotel suite, I couldn't help but realize that life was imitating art, or perhaps it was history itself.

After all, I had become his parents. August was running away from that, and for good reason. But I was the example.

Divorced twice, married twice, and lost beyond all recognition.

Because he was the love of my life.

And I knew if things went the way that history tended to, I would be left in the cold after mistake after mistake. And it would be all my fault.

It would be easier if I walked away now and didn't let myself get hurt. Only that's not how things went.

It couldn't be.

Not when I knew that even if we walked away now and just became friends, it was still going to hurt. Because I was beyond in love with this man. So there would be no protecting myself in the end.

There couldn't be.

"Knock, knock."

I looked over my shoulder and saw the man in question staring at me.

He had on gray suit pants and a white button-down. He looked gorgeous, all sleek, and strong.

I loved him. And I kept repeating that to myself because I knew if I didn't, I would run away out of fear.

But maybe, fighting for something stronger than myself and my own fear was the important part.

After all, I still didn't know why he had walked away in the first place. And I was so afraid to ask because if I did, maybe he would walk away again. Or maybe I would realize that it was my turn.

But I pushed those thoughts from my mind, as I needed to focus on what was in front of me.

"I thought you said you were getting ready?" I asked, in my most prim tone.

He just raised a brow, before leaning against the doorway. When he folded his hands over his chest, his forearms looking hot as hell, I nearly swallowed my tongue.

There was just something far too sexy about a man leaning in a doorway and looking far too casual.

"I just have to put on my tie and suit jacket. I'm ready to go. What about you?"

I looked down at my silk robe, and then at my hair still piled on the top of my head.

"Not even close. But I have a couple of hours before we have to be down for the wedding and cocktails. I thought you wanted to get with your brothers early though. Your parents had something in mind?"

It was odd to think that we were here for their wedding. I hadn't been to either of their other ones, and if I remembered right, August hadn't even been to his parents' second wedding. He had been grounded and hadn't wanted to go at all.

What a crock of shit. His parents had tried to break down his family.

"Well, Mom and Dad decided that they wanted to have time for just the two of them, rather than with us. So they're doing their pre-wedding ritual, not that I ever want to know what that is." He visibly shuddered, and I winced.

"Do you think it's something that they've done before every wedding? Or maybe it's like a lighting of a candle ceremony."

"These are questions I don't have answers to, nor do I want to think about ever again."

"I'm sorry," I said softly.

He shrugged. "There's nothing really we can do. Other than hope for the best. We're here because kicking the family out completely hasn't worked in the past."

"They seem like good grandparents though." I stood up then, setting my makeup brush to the side. I went to him, placing my hands on his chest. When he slid one of his up to grip my wrist, keeping me there, some part of me settled. He wasn't pushing me away.

"They're good grandparents. Odd that it surprises me, but they really are."

"But that doesn't give them a right to treat you as they did in the past. And it's a complicated situation that I know that you all are working on."

"Exactly. And I know one day we'll figure it out. Whether it be they're out of our lives completely, or they become the greatest grandparents ever. However, after this? I'm done. I don't want to have to try with them much longer. And if that makes me a bad son, then it does."

I put my free hand up over his cheek, cupping it. "That doesn't make you a bad son. It makes you someone who's finally protecting himself."

"I don't think I did a very good job of it in the past. But I'm going to protect you, okay?"

I froze, blinking up at him.

"What do you mean?" I asked softly.

"I know my parents haven't had much to do with us in the past." He paused. "Whatever us is."

That wasn't ominous at all.

"But I haven't done a very good job of making sure that you're safe in whatever this freaking family may be."

"Your parents have never bothered me." I lifted my chin and met his gaze. "They don't know me. And frankly they don't know you. But they have never bothered me and I'm fine with that."

"I don't know if that's a good thing or a bad thing?" He frowned. "I wasn't really good to you before."

My heart did that little quickstep, and I shook my head. "Let's just focus on today, okay? And the future."

I wasn't sure if I wanted to investigate the past. Neither one of us were ready to go there. Especially not on a day like today when the past seemed to be wrapping its claws around our throats. It didn't matter that it was selfish and probably weak of me, but I didn't want that. I just wanted now.

For once, as a person who spent most of her days thinking about the future, I wasn't going to think about it.

"You know, if you want, I can start the car, and we can make our way out. You don't have to protect me from your parents. They don't even know I exist."

And oddly that didn't give me pang of hurt. After all, if I had been in his parents' vicinity back when we had first been married, maybe things would have been different. Most likely for the worse. Because I saw day in and day out what their inactions and reactions did to him.

You couldn't blame your parents for everything, I knew that, but some parts you could. The way that my mother tried to control my life and push me into a box of her own making had forced me to make decisions that I might not have otherwise at the time.

Namely getting married not once, but twice. The first because my mother had said no, and she had resented me for it, the other because I had thought I'd been ready, and it had somehow made her happy. Why I had thought that would have been important at all, I didn't know, but there was no turning back from that. Jacob was over, and my relationship with my mother needed to be over soon.

"I'm sorry for bringing you into all this. It really doesn't make much sense, does it? The whole getting married multiple times and splitting up your kids throughout their whole life? I don't understand them."

I held back my frown considering his thoughts were on the same path as mine, and yet, not truly. Not when I was down another path as well. Because I wasn't sure if August saw himself in them. When it was all I could do not to see my own life and choices there.

"Well, it seems today we're just going to eat some cake, drink some champagne, and try to hope for the best. There's nothing else you can really do, is there?"

He shook his head, his hands falling from mine, so they were on my hips. I sighed and leaned into him.

"Maybe we should just run away. They won't even notice I'm gone."

I snorted. "I'm pretty sure they'll notice. They may be very much into each other, but they're going to notice if their son isn't there."

"They've got two other sons, a daughter, and a couple of grandkids. Not sure they need me."

"Well, if that's the case, let me go put on some pants and I'll start up the car."

He let out a grumbling noise, his hands sliding up my bare thigh. I moaned, sliding my thighs together.

"Why the hell aren't you wearing panties?" He groaned, his hand moving to cup my bare ass.

"I will be wearing panties when I put on my dress. But I'm just wearing my robe. And it's the two of us. I didn't feel like putting on clothes."

He leaned back a little, his hands still on my ass, spreading me slightly so his finger played between my cheeks. And then his other hand moved up to tug on the top of my robe, baring one breast.

"Well, it seems that somebody wanted to be a little naughty."

I rolled my eyes, even as my core pulsed, and my nipples pebbled. "There was nothing naughty about it. Just getting ready for the day."

"Or maybe you're just ready for me. You know, to keep my mind off things." And when his fingers slid between my legs, dipping inside me, I let my head fall back, groaning.

"August, we don't have time."

"I can be quick. Just a quick snack. They'll never know."

He leaned down, sucked one nipple into his mouth.

I moaned, my hands digging into his shirt. "I'll ruin your clothes."

"I'll be good. Don't worry."

And then he was on his knees, my robe long gone, and I was straddling his face. His tongue slid along my entrance, one lick, then another. I gripped the edge of the door, keeping myself steady as he held my thighs in his hands and began to lick at me as if he were a man starving.

"You're so fucking sweet. Soft."

He slid his hands along the inner creases of my

thighs, his thumbs playing with my lower lips, then my clit. When his fingers pressed deep inside me and curled to find that one bundle of nerves that always made everything go white, my toes curled, and I let out a shocked breath.

"August."

"That's it. Say my name."

He went back to lapping at me, using his other finger to play with my ass, sliding in and out, the sensation all too much. When I came, toes curling, he caught me as I fell. And then I was somehow on my knees, the sound of his belt undoing hitting my ears in such a way that I had to arch my back.

"There it is, you're all ready for me. Like a good little girl."

"Just shut up and fuck me already."

"As my lady wishes."

He slid into me in one thrust, his cock thick and long deep inside me, stretching me.

The feel of his pants against my bare thighs was a sensation unfamiliar, and yet so thrilling that it nearly sent me over the edge. He had my hips in his hands, holding me tightly, but not oh so gently. And when he slammed into me again and again, I met him thrust for thrust, my ass in the air as I continued to want more.

When I was nearly there, needing to come again, he

pulled out of me, and then went back to kneeling behind me.

"What are you..." I couldn't finish the sentence, because then his mouth was on me, and he was licking me up, one lick, then a second. He ate me from behind, devouring me, and I just pushed my ass back to his face, needing him.

I didn't want to think about words and forevers and where we were going after this. I just wanted this moment.

We didn't have to have feelings or thoughts or any future promises. We just needed this moment.

Because if there was anything we were ever good at, it was this.

Fucking and pretending.

He stood up, his pants below his ass, he pulled me with him, and then pressed my back against the wall. I lifted my legs, holding onto him for purchase, and then he was slamming into me, my legs wrapped around his waist. I met him move for move, needing him. He lowered his head slightly, lapping at my nipples, before taking my mouth again, and I was tugging on his shirt, knowing I was leaving creases. But I didn't care.

I just needed him in that moment.

When he came, moaning my name into my mouth, I ignored the tears sliding down my cheeks.

Because I didn't want this to end. Even though I knew it had to. I couldn't let this end.

I needed to tell him I loved him. That I wanted him. That I wasn't afraid that he would leave.

But I knew that was a lie.

When he leaned back and frowned, I quickly went to wipe my face, but he grabbed my wrist.

"What's wrong? Did I hurt you? Paise..."

I smiled at him then, the sound of my nickname on his lips bringing me to tears once again.

Why couldn't this be forever? Why did I feel as if I was losing who I had once been?

Why hadn't I been enough before?

And why did I feel as if I were to ask the question, I wouldn't find out the answer that I would want.

"I just wasn't expecting this to happen this morning."

He studied my face, and while I hadn't lied, I hadn't told him the whole truth. "Paise."

"We need to get you ready. I'm glad I brought you a second shirt. Just in case the lighting of the room was not perfect for the shirt you had before."

He rolled his eyes at me, and I was grateful that I had distracted him with my nonsense.

"You made me bring two shirts because you were afraid that I would match? They're both white."

"One is ivory, the other is pale snow. There's a difference."

He was still balls deep within me, his cock pulsing. This was such a ridiculous conversation, but anything not to have feelings in that moment.

But he kissed me softly, and then pulled out of me. I used my robe to clean up after both of us, and then I quickly showered without getting my hair wet, knowing he would change, and we only had a few minutes before we had to be down for cocktails.

I felt sore in all the best ways, but my heart felt just as much.

We would need to talk, something we were good at avoiding. I put my hair in a quick updo that would hide any crinkles from his hands, redid my makeup to hide the blushing, and was grateful that my dress went down to the floor to hide the bruising around my thighs. The bruising that I had begged for because I loved when he held me hard.

August never hurt me in that way. Only in the ways that we didn't speak of. But he wasn't hurting me now. We hadn't made any promises. We hadn't told ourselves what we might want in the future.

And so why would I be hurt?

If there was no future here, I didn't have to fall off into a precipice. And if there was a future, as long as I didn't fall into the abyss without looking back, I would be safe.

Only I knew I was lying to myself.

"You look breathtaking."

I looked over at August then and swallowed hard. He had put on his tie and suit jacket and looked as if he had not a care in the world.

My red hair fell in waves in the front and was tied up in the back, and it was as good as it was going to get.

I had chosen a soft lilac dress that should have clashed with my hair but hadn't. It was just a dress. Because no matter what I wore, I would still wear his marks on my flesh. The marks I had begged for. So there lay the difference.

"You look handsome yourself. And you don't look as if you just fucked me hard against the wall."

"But I'll know. And that's all that matters."

"And the wall will know. I'm sure they say if only walls could talk is a thing, but I'm glad they don't. Let's just keep that between ourselves."

His gaze went to my mouth, and he shook his head.

My hand went to my lips, and I frowned. "What? Do I have lipstick on my teeth?"

"No, but your lips are swollen. So I'm pretty sure they're going to figure out what happened."

I rolled my eyes and grabbed my clutch before taking his outstretched hand.

"If they hadn't noticed that my lips had been swollen last night after sucking your cock for a good twenty minutes, they're not going to know now."

"Oh, I'm pretty sure they knew."

That made me nearly trip over my feet.

"What?"

"Because I looked so smug. And spent. Because you sure do know how to wring out a man."

I was laughing as we opened the door, meeting the others in the hallway.

When everyone smiled at us, gazes curious, and yet so full of hope that it worried me, I told myself not to worry. After all, they told us that it was the hope that killed you, but maybe I just needed to trust.

Maybe he wouldn't leave.

Maybe it would be okay.

And as we sat down at the wedding and watched August's parents vow to love each other to eternity once again, he held my hand, and I squeezed back. He was the one who needed my strength, and I would be there.

The tableau of watching a couple who had broken the hearts of their children more than once wasn't lost on me.

I wouldn't tell myself that if they could fall in love again and trust again, I could as well.

Because that would be dishonest to everyone in this situation.

Especially to me.

"I have fought through Valhalla for you my darling, and I will fight through eternity to be by your side. The two of us against the world."

August's father began to wax poetic nonsense, as August's mother cried happy tears, and I stole a look at the man that I loved.

His jaw was tight, and he held onto my hand in such a firm grip I knew he probably didn't even realize he was doing it.

Just the two of them against the world.

As if they hadn't torn through their family countless times in order to make it so.

August was not like his parents in any way. I knew that, and I hoped he did too.

But I saw the worry on his face. Even as I wanted to trust.

Maybe I was seeing too much.

Or maybe, that mistake I told myself not to see in the mirror cried out an agony.

Either way, I held onto his hand and watched this

farce of a wedding, and told myself that this was not the path, nor the history I was doomed to repeat.

Chapter Fifteen

August

"So when does the drinking start?" Luca asked, and I stared over at the bar, willing it to open.

"Who knows? I thought we were having cocktail hour before the wedding, just so I could get through the ceremony, and yet here we are, dry as a bone."

"Did I tell you she asked me to provide the alcohol for the event because I own a bar?" Heath asked, and both Luca and I gave him a look.

"Are you serious?"

"Yep. It doesn't matter that it's a small wedding or not. They wanted free booze, and food for that matter. I told them that we didn't cater that way and didn't have the ability. And once again I'm the asshole. I'm shocked. Aren't you? With me, the asshole of the family."

"I'm pretty sure I'm the asshole. Didn't we already agree to this?" I asked, feeling as if this had all been another fucking mistake.

"Did you hear those vows?" Luca whispered, as other people milled about.

It surprised me that our folks had even wanted to get married in Colorado, since they didn't even live here. But their kids did, so we were just going with what they wanted. Nothing my parents did ever made sense and hadn't since I could remember.

I hated the fact that we were here at all, but we were giving them one last chance, because we were family, and they had been trying. They had been better for the past year.

They had been caring with the kids, and while yes, they had been selfish in some ways, they hadn't outright hurt us. And what a low fucking bar that was.

"If anyone's the asshole, we know it's not one of us," Luca said softly.

"I hope you're talking about Mom and Dad, and not our lovely dear sister," I said as I lifted my chin toward Greer. She was in the middle of an urgent discussion with her husbands, and I had a feeling they would be leaving soon. Our parents still couldn't quite get over the fact that their baby girl was in a poly relationship. Sometimes they were perfectly okay with it, and at other times they acted as if it was the oddest thing in the world. And somehow my parents had made friends in this state and there were over one hundred people at this wedding. Some of them were great and treated my family with respect. Others? Not so much.

I had already had to stare down a woman with arched eyebrows as she glared at my sister. Nobody was going to hurt my baby sister's feelings.

Thankfully I knew that she wasn't going to be staying long. There was no reason for her to.

But I didn't know why I was still there. I just wanted to go.

I wasn't sure why I had invited Paisley. A weak moment? Maybe the fact I had just wanted her. We'd stayed at the event hotel the night before because my parents had wanted us to have dinner there and the timing just worked out. It had been nice, waking up again with Paisley in my arms. I had had to deal with a few school board things over email that morning, and Paisley had dealt with a thousand things at once being the multi-business owner that she was, making millions while sometimes never sleeping.

She was brilliant, hardworking, and I knew still getting over her divorce.

But I had wanted her by my side so I wouldn't have to deal with this alone.

I was so selfish.

"So, you and Paisley seem to be doing well." I looked over at Heath, and wondered if that twin magic thing had happened again and he could read my mind.

He just gave me a curious look, as Luca stared at me as well, and I shrugged.

"We're just friends."

"I don't think I ever did that with my friend before," Luca said, and I glared at him.

"Weren't you fake dating your best friend?" I asked, speaking of Addison.

"Yeah, and I married her. Because I love her. So, want to do that again?"

I rolled my eyes, and nearly let out a cheer when the bar opened. I slid away from my brothers and was first in line to get a glass of whiskey, and because I was gracious, I got two more for my brothers.

I handed the glasses over to them, before lifting mine in salute and taking a sip.

I cringed at the taste, though it wasn't the worst whiskey I'd ever had, but it was fine. We would leave the next day, and I wouldn't have to deal with this much longer.

Whatever this was.

"So you're really not going to talk about Paisley. I like the two of you together." I glared at Heath, but he continued anyway. "It's okay if you guys are casual, or just figuring things out, but don't lie to yourself and say you're just friends. I see the way that you look at her, the way that you have always looked at her. Be truthful about it. Figure out what you want, and make it happen. Because she looks at you the same way, bro."

"We're not like that. We tried that before, and it didn't work." I gestured around the mockery of a wedding with my whiskey glass. "Look what happens when you believe it can work repeatedly. It doesn't."

"You were nothing like our parents," Luca whispered, and I was grateful that he whispered, considering that there were so many of their friends around us.

"Even so, history repeats itself."

"With them. You got married when you were too young, fine. But you guys aren't young kids anymore. You guys are adults, with jobs, careers, and futures. You have people that like you separately and together. Figure it out, August. You're not our parents."

I shook my head and downed the rest of my glass.

"I'm going to go find Paisley. I left her alone too long even though I'm the one who dragged her here."

"She's off with our wives having girl time. You may have dragged her up here, but she's still with her friends."

And that was the problem. Because these were her friends. My family. I was such an asshole.

I moved past the partygoers, ignoring my brothers' shouts for me, and made my way to Paisley. I just needed to figure things out. But as I rounded the corner, everything shifted once again.

"I saw the way that you were looking at him." My dad.

"So? You had your hands on Nancy's ass," my mother spat.

My parents stood in front of each other, her in a lacy ivory dress, my father in a tan suit, and couldn't help but wonder once again why I was here.

Their faces were pressed toward one another as they yelled, before they would move back and begin to pace. They were still at their goddamn wedding, still wearing their wedding shoes and wedding rings. It had just been forty-five minutes since they had vowed to love each other above all else—including their own kids. But no, they couldn't even handle forty-five minutes before they realized that they had made a mistake.

You could've colored me shocked.

"I wasn't dancing with Nancy. I was just making sure she found her seat since she was drunk."

"You had your hands on her last year."

"Because we were on a break."

"Don't bring that TV show logic here. I don't care if we were on a break, and we were sleeping with other people. We also had Nancy in our bed together if you don't remember that. And you're still touching her?"

There were some things a son shouldn't know. Like the fact that apparently my parents sometimes had an open relationship. Which I wasn't going to judge, but the fact that they sometimes judged their daughter for having a poly, closed relationship where the three people loved each other with every ounce of their beings?

No, I was done. So done.

"If you guys are going to keep yelling at each other and pushing out wild accusations, I would do it a little quieter before your guests hear. They can still take your wedding gifts back, and I'm pretty sure that's why you keep getting married. For the free shit."

"August. We didn't see you there," Mom said, as she gripped my father's hand out of solidarity or perhaps warning. I didn't know, and I didn't care.

"I'm headed out. I wish you guys the next few seconds of marital bliss because I'm not quite sure it's going to last that much longer. But thank you for reminding me what happens when you keep trying again. What's the old saying that the first mistake is on someone else and the second mistake's on you? Or maybe it's the repeated trying that makes you a fucking idiot."

"August, that's no way to speak to your parents."

"You stopped being our parents a long time ago. I don't know why we keep trying. Good luck in whatever farce of a relationship you guys think you have. But all I can see are two people who keep trying and keep fighting without realizing that you guys weren't meant to be."

"That's not true. I love your father."

"Even with the fact that he's fucking Nancy?"

"Watch your mouth, August," my dad snapped.

"You know what, you're right. It isn't any of my business. But if you keep screaming it so that the guests hear, it's going to be their business. And Nancy's business. And I'm pretty sure Nancy is married, right? Again, not my fucking business. But maybe you want to quiet down just in case the kids that still somewhat like you don't overhear. Because I'm done."

And with that, I moved down the path, my shoulders tense.

I was done. Done with the parents that continued to show me exactly what happened when you tried to cover up your mistakes.

They pretended to love each other, and continued to

vow one another, and they couldn't even last five minutes.

Why the hell was I still trying with someone that I couldn't stop fighting before? I wasn't going to become my parents.

I was the rebound in Paisley's life. Maybe I was even the rebound to myself. So I was going to do the one thing that I could do.

Set her free, before we ended up like my parents.

Hating each other at our own wedding.

I turned round the corner, and my heart stopped as I saw her standing there, phone in hand, her lavender dress glowing under the lights. Her hair had fallen out of the bun and was now flowing over her shoulders and down her back. She was like a fae goddess, gorgeous with high cheekbones and stunning curves. And she wasn't for me.

If I wanted to keep Paisley happy, I had to do what was best for both of us.

Because this wasn't going to work. We couldn't even talk about why it wasn't going to work.

So I would walk away. And leave her some sense of dignity. Leave her with her friends.

Because I wouldn't let her become what I had just seen.

She looked up at me then, smiling so bright that her

eyes shined under the lights. It was like a kick to the gut, but I had to be stronger.

"Hey. Sorry, that was a work call. You know my job. Never really ends." She winced. "Not the greatest thing to say when I'm trying to find a work/life balance." She shook her head and put on a bright smile. "Hi, there. It was a beautiful wedding. Albeit odd vows."

I stared off into the distance, giving her a one-armed shrug. "Well, my parents are already fighting and screaming divorce, so this might be the shortest marriage ever."

She blinked at me, her mouth dropping. "Are you serious? No. There's no way."

"Yes, way. I think they like fighting and drama more than they even like each other. I don't even care anymore."

"I'm sorry. About them. I know there's nothing you can do, but it still sucks."

I slid my hands in my pockets, afraid I would reach out and touch her. "There's nothing I can do about my parents. But there's something I can do now."

She paused in the action of sliding her phone into her small purse, that frown between her eyes deepening.

"August? What are you talking about?"

"I shouldn't have brought you here. I did it because I am selfish. Because I didn't want to be the sole brother alone without a date. But I realized I made a mistake. That I was leading both of us on."

Her chin lifted slightly in that instant, and I saw the Paisley I had known since I had moved here before everything had shifted. The same Paisley who had told me she was marrying Jacob and was finally with a man who would love her for who she was.

That had turned out to be a lie, but then again, I was just as good at lying to myself, it seemed.

This was for the best. It would keep her safe from my family, and from the blood that ran in my veins. Because there was only so much happiness that could be bled from a stone. My siblings had all found their happy ever afters, but I had thrown mine away once, and I didn't deserve it again. Paisley would thrive without me, something we both knew had to be true.

I just had to be the smarter person.

"I'm sorry, I don't think I heard you correctly. Are you telling me that you didn't want me here?"

"It's not that. It's nice what we've had. It's good relaxation. I've been a nice rebound for you. But before it goes any further, before either one of us hurts another person, I think it'd be good if we just back off. End it. A clean break so that way you can still hang out with Devney, Greer, and Addison, and you don't feel like you have to lose them too."

It felt as if there were sawdust in my mouth as I spoke, but this was for the best. Because one day soon Paisley would realize how much better she was than me, and we would end up like my parents, and she'd be alone.

And I'd do anything not to make that happen.

I ignored the voice in my head that said that this was a mistake. That me being with her wouldn't let her be alone, but what would happen when she saw me for the real person I was.

No, this was for the best.

There were two feet between us, but it might as well have been the Grand Canyon. It was a gulf, broken up into a shattering cavern that made no logical sense.

A single tear slid down her face, reminding me of that tear from before. The one that I knew had been about me.

"Paise."

"No. No." She shook her head but didn't wipe the tear. Instead she let another fall.

She hadn't cried the first time that I had left. The first time that I had broken both of us.

That was a change.

"You don't get to call me Paise. And you don't get to pretend that this is about protecting me. You don't get to call me a rebound or call yourself one. I'll take the blame for not asking why you broke everything before, but I don't want answers right now. Not when I'm wearing another dress, and I can hear laughter behind us. Laughter and happiness for a wedding that probably won't amount to anything. So fine. Be a coward. Walk away again. Because I knew it."

I frowned, taking a step forward. But she took one step back, holding her hands out.

"No. No. Do you want me to fight and yell for you? Do you want me to beg you to stay? Because we both know I won't do that. Not when you have clearly already made up your mind. You are not your parents. Just like I'm not my bitch of a mother. But here I am, acting the shrew for this little tableau. Break it off, or perhaps we don't have to break it off since there was never a label to this. But I knew it," she repeated, "I knew I wasn't enough. I was never going to be the one to show you that you weren't your parents. Your brothers and sister and their families weren't enough either. That's on you. So I'm not going to yell at you. I'm not going to be your mother. I'm not going to fight. I'm not going to be your father. I'm just going to be me. The person you pushed away. *Twice*."

And with that she turned on her heel and walked toward our rooms.

And I let her go.

Again.

This was for the best.

Before she fell in love with me, before I broke her heart, this was for the best.

So why did it feel like I'd once again ruined everything?

Chapter Sixteen

Paisley

"Jessa, do you have the contract for the Hoovers?" I asked, not noticing that my voice had become so brittle, so encased with ice, I had become the one thing that I had been afraid of for so long.

The ice queen personified. She was back.

But I was tired. Oh so tired.

"Right on it, Paisley. Is there anything else?"

I let out a breath, telling myself to calm down, and answered. "No, that's it. Thank you."

"No problem."

Was that pity in her voice? Or just worry?

I wasn't sure anymore. After all, I was not even sure what everyone knew.

News of Jacob's engagement had hit the cycles

again. So now I was not just the woman left behind, I was now the scorned woman. Because with that engagement, came the lovely stories of why things had come so quickly.

I was the one he cheated on, and of course, it had to be something that I had done. It couldn't be that Jacob couldn't keep his dick in his pants. No, he had to be the one that had fallen because I couldn't be good enough for him. I wasn't quite sure what PR teams that Jacob's family were using right then, but it was a little ridiculous how quick they were on top of things. It wasn't affecting my business as of yet, and I knew that people who would think that I couldn't handle my business because he'd cheated on me weren't people I wanted to work with anyway.

Of course it was all easier said than done because people knew.

They knew that once again I wasn't good enough.

I was so done.

Addison and Paisley were both offsite today, both of them working from home since the girls had the sniffles. I had told them to just take the day off, but they had said they wanted to work on a few projects.

And unlike the rest of the company, they knew that it wasn't Jacob on my mind.

No, it was the man who had left me again.

Should I have fought for him? For what. He had clearly made up his mind. Me baring my soul and telling him that I loved him wouldn't save anything. It made me feel like a coward.

I hadn't fought for Jacob because there was nothing to fight for.

I hadn't fought for August the first time because I thought I hadn't been enough. Only I hadn't fought *again*. I should have. But I hadn't. Because it was easier to walk away and pretend. This time I could even tell myself I had done the right thing because he had done it first.

He had done what he had always done. Made me feel left behind, less than. I mean, it wasn't as if I should be shocked about this new revelation. I had even expected it. I had nearly written it down in stone that I was not good enough for him.

"Get it together, Paisley," I whispered to myself.

Wallowing in the same feelings and repeating the same phrases in my mind repeatedly wasn't going to help.

So instead, I went to work. It was what I was good at.

I was better off doing things alone. Yes, I had friends, friends that would remind me of the time that I had fallen in love, not once, but twice with the wrong man. But I could still have them in my life. When they reached out to me. I would help when they needed their Auntie Paisley, but I wouldn't encroach.

Because it was better to do things on my own where people wouldn't have to disappoint me. I could travel on my own, join a club for singles where they wouldn't date each other. One where the bylaws meant that it was just so you would have company if you needed it.

I had already researched travel sites on traveling alone, and how to walk through cities and national parks by yourself and be safe. I had already searched different platforms where you wouldn't have the couples' tax—where some things were booked as occupancy of two like cruises, and a single person got screwed over.

So no, I would be fine. No one needed to know that I was dying inside and waiting to be left once again.

I had a career that I excelled at. I had a platform I could use for good. And I had work that could fulfill me. I had money that could take me places and let me visit places. And I would have Paisley and Addison and their families when they needed me.

I didn't need anyone else.

Needing and loving other people just broke your heart in the end when they left you. Relying on others just reminded you that you could only rely on yourself.

Because when you failed, you only disappointed your-self and that was something that I was used to.

I let out a breath and went back to work. The sale of the matchmaking company to the original owner's wishes was now complete. There were a few little snickers from some organizations about the fact that I couldn't keep a man and would need that matchmaking service, but that didn't matter in the end.

I would do what I did best, be the ice queen of busi-nesswomen, walk on my stiletto heels, and be alone.

It was safer.

My fingers slid across the keys as I answered another email, my phone ringing once again as my assistant forwarded a call, and I kept going.

I wouldn't think about the fact that August hadn't wanted forever. And I had for just one instant, thought I could trust that. But he hadn't wanted forever before and wouldn't tell me why. So why would I have to be the one to get on my knees and ask?

I ended the call with a reporter, this time about a charity organization I was running, and went to work on the next gala. Each charity gala I did brought in thou-sands, sometimes hundreds of thousands for specific charities. I worked my ass off on them, and because I didn't have a social life now, I could continue to work my ass off.

Maybe I would get back in those jeans and sparkly shoes of mine and go line dancing again, albeit this time sober. And maybe I would just enjoy the town on my own. There were thousands of things I hadn't done yet, and I was no longer waiting for a man or a family to make that happen.

I went back to work, as lunch passed, and people came in and out of my office. When my phone buzzed, I looked down, and my heart ached. I hated the fact that it did. Because it wasn't going to be him, of course it wasn't going to be, but it was someone close.

Devney: *Girls' night this weekend?*

Addison: *Why are you even asking? The answer is yes.*

I pressed my lips together, before letting out a breath.

Me: *I have that deadline for the gala coming up, and I'm planning a trip. But maybe next time? Rain check?*

Devney: *Oh. We can help you with the gala if you want.*

Addison: *Of course we're going to help you with the gala, but what you're also going to do is freaking go with us to girls' night. You don't get to hide.*

I loved and hated my friends.

Me: *I'm not hiding. I'm working. And I do have a*

trip coming up. I'm okay, girls. You don't have to worry about me.

Addison: *Maybe we want you to worry about us. Because I'm selfish.*

My lips twitched and I shook my head even though my two best friends couldn't see me.

Me: *You couldn't be selfish.*

Addison: *I could try.*

Devney: *We can all try. We can be selfish together. I think that sort of negates the process.*

Me: *I love you both. Let me get back to work. And I'll think about it.*

But I wouldn't. I would join them on another day. When the hurt wasn't too fresh. When I got through the agonizing pain part of grief and hit the anger part. Yes, anger would be good. And as if I had summoned my own anger, my mother and Jacob walked through the door.

I set my palms down on my desk on either side of my keyboard, and stared at two people that I honestly hated. I didn't like the word hate because it created a sense of ownership in my opinion, but hate felt good.

"You don't need to bother closing the door, Jacob, because you will be leaving right away." I stood up, my chin lifted, as I stared at my mother and my ex-husband, wondering why they were even here. And I was sure I wasn't going to like the answer.

"Paisley, we are here as a show of unity."

I held up my hand and shook my head. "No. You're not. You're here with some form of a scheme that doesn't make any sense." I turned to Jacob. "Your engagement was just announced. Why are you in the office of your ex-wife? With my mother? What kind of bullshit did the two of you think you could work together in order to shine your profiles simultaneously? The cheating is already out, but you're a politician. We're used to it."

"Paisley," my mother snapped. "Look what you're giving up with your selfishness and coldness. There is so much out there for you and so much you can offer these propositions. You will sit down and listen. I am your mother. I sacrificed *everything* for you. You will listen to me."

I wasn't even sure my mother believed the words coming out of her mouth at this point. "No. I'm done. I don't know what you two think you're going to accomplish by being in this room, but it literally makes no sense to me right now. So just leave. I don't want you here." I turned to her, my shoulders straight. "And you *never* sacrificed for me. Not in the end. You said you did, but no, you used me. All of my life I've been your ticket. We had money growing up, but it was never enough. We had a family between the two of us, or at least we could have, but it was never enough. I played beauty queen and prodigy for you. I was a poet and an ice princess for you. But when I wanted to find my own way, to be myself, you took that from me. You made me feel like I was nothing. So I'm done, Mother. I've been done for a while but you never listened. I moved away from you, and you followed. Leave. Leave and cut the ties. It's beyond time."

"How could you say those things to me?" my mother asked, her voice full of shock. I could almost imagine it was real.

"I should have said them a long time ago." I turned to Jacob. "Go home. To your next wife or whatever decision you decide to make. But I won't be part of it."

"Lydia and I will not be getting married."

I blinked for a moment, trying to come up with words to Jacob's exclamation, but instead I just threw my head back and laughed. It was a good laugh, one of humor and sarcasm with a little bit of hatred. Oh, there was that anger, it was starting to bubble up. I had missed it.

"Oh, that's rich. Oh wait, *she's* the rich one. Wasn't she?"

"It's a setback for the Bartons for sure," my mother

said, trying her best to sound reasonable. "However, there are options."

"The Bartons are richer than God in their opinion, isn't that what your mother always said, Jacob?"

Jacob cleared his throat, looking far more awkward than I'd seen him in the past. Interesting and not unpleasant. "We are fine financially, but as news of the broken engagement will hit news waves by tomorrow, your mother and I have come up with a new platform."

"What? That you and I have decided to get back together? How on earth is that going to help you? You flip-flopping between wives isn't going to help you stay firm on your political stances. That's not how things work. And I'm not going along with it."

"You will. For the good of the family."

I rounded on my mother, moving along the side of my desk. "Are you serious right now? What family? Dad is gone. You hate me other than what I can do for you. I'm not going to be your prom queen. I'm not going to be Little Miss Oregon. Just leave. I'm not going into whatever schemes you think you need."

"I made you who you are today," my mother barked. "Without me, you would have no ambition. I was the one that pushed you for those scholarships, for those connections. If you had done what you had wanted to all those years ago, you wouldn't have this business. Those business deals would have ended before they'd even begun if you had stayed with that little teacher. If he hadn't come to the realization that you needed someone stronger like Jacob. Now he needs you, and you need him, and you could be the power couple of the century. Yes, there was that little bump of divorce, but you could use it to talk about family connections and finding love after pain. We have ways."

My mother and Jacob kept rambling, but things started to click. Things that should have clicked long ago. Yet I hadn't thought that August would have let them. Or perhaps, I hadn't given my mother that much credit.

"What did you say to August all those years ago?" I asked, my voice oddly strong even though I was screaming inside.

My mother stiffened, as if she hadn't realized she had let those words slip. "Nothing. He left you, and that was great. It was good for us."

She was lying and I needed to know why. "What did you say to him to make him leave me?" I was guessing at this, but I had a horrible sinking feeling.

"If I could have said anything to him to make him leave, he would've been a little weakling."

I shook my head. "No. Because he loved me. What

did you say to him that he had to protect me?" I asked, guessing, and yet fearing.

"Oh, stop being such a drama queen," Jacob snarled, and I whirled on him.

"Excuse me? You don't get to say anything. You get to leave here and go grovel back to your other fiancée, or just leave in general. I don't want to see you again. In fact if you set foot on these premises again, I'm filing for a restraining order. How will that do for your publicity and your pretty little family?."

"You wouldn't dare."

"Watch me," I said so swiftly that he took a step back. And then I whirled once again on my mother. "What did you do?"

She lifted her chin in a gesture that reminded me so much of myself that bile rose in my throat. "What had to be done. If you would like the details, you can talk to him. But just know he was the one who left. And from what I hear, he left again. You don't need a weak man."

"I don't want to see you again. You know nothing about August. Nothing about me. I'm done being your puppet. If you want Jacob and his money so much, you marry him." I laughed then, pure joy writhing through me. "Oh yes. Be the cougar that you've always wanted to be and fuck my ex-husband. I don't care what you do.

Maybe it'll be good for you, Jacob. Someone to mother you when I was never going to be that person. And my mom can have the connections she wants. I don't care. Just get out of my office, get out of my life, and never speak with me again. I'm done." I went to the door and opened it, gesturing for them both to leave. "I'll call security right now. To get you both. Neither one of you is welcome in my office, my life, or in my general vicinity. And, Mother? I will find out what you said to August. And I will deal with him later. But you do not get to dictate my life ever again. I should have stood up for myself long before this. And that's shame on me. But shame on you for thinking you could ever try it again. Get the fuck out."

I hadn't realized that people were staring, until a couple of people let out claps and a holler, and I nodded at them, before glaring back at Jacob and my mother. "Well?" I asked, gesturing once again.

Heads high, both walked out the door, and I knew that I would probably see them again, but I would deal with it legally.

I was done. Oh so done.

"Jessa, can you hold my calls for the day and change my meetings? I have to go fix something."

"Go get him," she said, and I snorted.

"No, I'm not quite sure that's going to happen, but I

need answers. And I'm done being the sideshow for the day."

"It has been getting quite boring here," Arnold, one of the partners said as he walked by.

I sighed and grabbed my purse. "I'll call everyone soon about the gala, but I need to go yell at someone else."

"We won't warn Addison and Devney though," Jessa said. "Just so they don't warn him."

I held back a snort. It seemed that I wasn't being as discreet as I'd thought. Everyone knew my business, but maybe I'd use that for good. Because I was going to get the truth out of August even if I had to growl it out of him. "That sounds like a plan."

It was a non-school day. I knew that it was a teacher holiday, so I didn't know where he was. I also didn't want to warn him with a phone call. Since he wasn't at the house, I drove to Heath's bar. All of the extra driving time gave me time to figure out what to say. Only I had no idea how to begin. I'd have to think of something soon. When I stomped through the front door, both Heath and Luca were there, and they stared at me, wide-eyed.

"Where is he?" I snapped, as all of Heath's customers looked at me. I should be embarrassed, but right then I was tired. Oh so tired.

Without a second beat, Luca answered, "He's in the family cabin." He frowned. "What's wrong, Paisley?"

"Nothing's wrong. I'm just finally standing up for myself and I'm done being set aside. I'm going to get him to tell me a few things before I yell at him and maybe push him off a mountain." I paused. "Scratch that, because I'm not going to get in trouble for premeditated anything."

Heath and Luca gave each other a look, before giving me broad smiles. "I'll text you the address, you should be able to get there in about an hour. We won't warn him."

I nodded tightly, eager and anxious to get started. "Good. Because I'm done waiting for when August thinks is a good time."

"Good for you. Go kick his ass," Luca said with a grin.

"I should have kicked his ass a long time ago."

"August is good about pretending that he has to be the sacrifice in our family. It never made any sense to me." Heath shook his head. "So you kick his ass, and then we'll all kick his ass as a family. What do you say?"

I smiled, feeling as if I wasn't alone. Something I should have realized all along. I had my friends—including the men in front of me—and I shouldn't have pushed them away all this time. "All I can say is that I'm going to fix this. Because it's what I do. And I should have remembered that long ago."

"Damn straight. I'll text the girls in the group chat," Luca said, pulling out his phone.

I rolled my eyes, and made my way back to the car, ignoring the cheers and claps from strangers I had a feeling I would never see again. Apparently, I was good at being the sideshow. But that was fine with me.

Because I was going to get the truth out of August. And then I would kick his ass.

And then I would tell him I loved him.

We would have to see what happened after that, but I hadn't gotten my second chance yet.

And it was about time I tried.

Chapter Seventeen

August

I zipped up my coat, shivering a bit, as the cold front began to blow through.

Of course, a winter storm not in the middle of winter was going to hit my cabin, but that was Colorado weather for you. You could have every single season in one day, and circle back. The forecast hadn't called for snow that morning, but now it seemed that some was on the way. I would be fine though. I had a backup generator, logs for the fireplace, and food and water to get me through. Even if I had to stay a couple of days if I got snowed in up here, I'd be fine. I had papers to grade, books to read, and people to avoid.

Namely my family.

I still couldn't quite believe that I had soberly and royally fucked up my life so badly.

I made my way back inside the cabin and was grateful that my family and I had gone in on it together. It wasn't one of the cabin McMansions that dotted the area, but it was a nice place that could hold most of our family. With the family growing leaps and bounds with new kids, one day it might not be big enough for all of us if we wanted something more than a sleeping bag, but it wasn't like we used this place together. For now, it was just an oasis. Or if you asked my brother, it was a place for me to hide from my dumb ass decisions.

Luca wasn't wrong about that.

I was the exact dumb ass that he called me.

I had been scared, unworthy, thinking with my past, and not my head, my heart, or even my dick. Maybe if I had been thinking with my dick, I wouldn't have made such monumentally stupid decisions. But alas, I hadn't.

So here I was, alone in a cabin with only my thoughts to keep me company.

And it was everything I deserved.

As soon as I had let her walk away, I knew that it was a mistake. But I couldn't take it back. That would just make me more of a damaging and hateful person than I had already become.

I wasn't a child. I wasn't worried about Paisley's mother ruining the business.

No, I had been worried about myself.

Worried about hurting the person that I loved, and then I ended up doing it anyway.

It made no sense, and I had been scared. Scared something had been real, and now I couldn't take it back.

I wouldn't be surprised if my family never talked to me again after realizing that this was permanent. They would take Paisley's side like they should, and maybe I would see them on holidays. If they let me. Maybe I could video chat with my nieces, so they would remember what Uncle August looked like. I frowned as I set down my backpack. I was a twin. They didn't need me, did they? Because they always had Heath. Meaning they could just say Uncle August looked like Heath and move on.

Hell. I was all my own disastrous making and there was no turning back.

I went outside, cup of tea in hand, and sat down on the porch to lament.

I just needed to think. To formulate a plan.

To just be.

When the Mercedes skittered up the path, its traction not that great up on this hill, I nearly dropped my mug. Instead, I set it on the porch railing, and clambered down the steps.

I already knew whose car it was, and while I wasn't

surprised at the red-haired woman that stormed out of the door, I was still damn surprised she was even here.

"August Cassidy. We are going to have a talk. Finally. And you're up in this remote cabin, so you can't run away from me again. There is no running. Only answers. Do you hear me?"

I blinked at the woman I loved, the woman I thought I would never see again, and swallowed hard.

"Paisley?" Maybe I was dreaming? Though I wasn't sure if I'd ever dreamed her so angry before. She moved forward, hair flying, and I held back a smile. Oh yeah, I'd dreamed her this angry before.

"Don't Paisley me. You know exactly who I am. Surprised to see me? Well, maybe because you left me, not once, but twice. I guess you should be a little surprised to see me. But anyway, fuck you. Fuck you, August Cassidy."

I held up my hands.

"Do you want some tea. A drink?"

"I don't want anything from you but answers." She folded her hands over her chest, as a strong wind hit, and I cursed.

"Come inside, Paise. It's getting cold." As the first snowflake dropped, Paisley glared up at it.

"Are you telling me there's going to be a storm? It is not winter."

"It's close to it. I mean, it's Colorado. You sort of just expect weather at all times."

"I am not being snowed in a cabin with you."

"Then I would get down the path right now before you get snowed in, though, I don't know if your Mercedes is going to make it. I have always loved that car." I whistled through my teeth, and she stomped toward me. She wasn't wearing weather appropriate clothing, and looked damn sexy when she was all fiery. But I would never say that misogynistic thing out loud. Especially not right now while she was fuming at me. I valued my life, and my balls.

"August. Why are you so scared? Just talk to me. After all this time, just talk to me. And then I'll go away and never ask you again. But now I'm the one standing up and trying to be strong. To be brave. But just tell me. Why did you leave all those years ago? What happened?"

"Let's go."

"No. Because we'll do something stupid like sleep together."

I raised a brow, and she just scowled at me.

"I know it's what we do. We get angry with each other, and we pretend that we're fine, and then we're not. Because in the end, we both are so good at avoiding our problems and real decisions, that we just fall into this pattern. And I'm not going to let it happen again. I fell into a pattern with my mother for so long, and standing up to her today? Standing up to her and Jacob and whatever nefarious plans that they had? It felt amazing."

"What the hell did they do? Are you okay?"

I was in front of her in a flash, checking her for marks and bruises. But I had a feeling it was only the emotional bruises that were left. I had caused my fair share of them.

"They came to me wanting, I don't know, for me to marry him again?"

Anger slammed into me. "Are you fucking kidding me?"

"That's what I said. I don't know what all their plans were, but they can work on them together. By themselves. I threatened restraining orders."

"Damn straight," I shouted, so fucking proud of her.

"I should have done it a long time ago. But I was so worried I'd screw something up. And it was hard to stand up to my mom. She might've been a terrible mother in some respects, but she did take care of me."

"That's like me saying because my dad kept us fed and housed that he was a good father when he was rarely around. Or the fact that my mother only showed up when she needed something. We don't have good parents, Paisley."

"I know that. You know that. But I'm not my mother. When are you going to realize that you are not your parents?"

I ran my hands over my face, even as the snow began to come down harder. Little flakes landed on her eyelashes, and I wanted to wipe them away, to keep her warm. But I had a feeling if I tried to do anything but tell her the absolute truth, she wouldn't let me.

Relief and worry warred within me. After so many years, I needed to tell her. About how cowardly I had been. Even trying to protect the woman that I loved. Even as the fear had been too much.

"You don't get to leave. You left before, and I'm done. We're going to talk this out. We got married because we loved each other. Yes, it was rash and it was quick and it might not have worked out anyway, but you just picked up everything and left. And I was so busy trying not to fall in love with you again this time, that I let it happen. I ignored everything that happened before so that way we would just not deal with the consequences or anything complicated. And I don't want to be that way. Talk to me."

"You are everything, Paisley."

"But I wasn't enough."

"Fuck that. You were *everything*. You were going to take over the world. Look at you now? You've been on the cover of *Forbes*. *Time Magazine*. You're literally one of the most powerful people in the world."

"Not really. I just have some good press sometimes. And as you've seen recently, I don't have good press *all* the time. I'm not powerful in the world but I do have power within my small circles. That's why not being able to have any power in my personal life is killing me."

"And I'm sorry for that. I'm sorry for being such a jackass."

"But why? Why did you leave?"

"Because you deserve more than some high school chemistry teacher. We were trying to figure out our jobs and our times to see each other, and I was just trying to find a place that was going to give me medical insurance."

She took a step back, nearly sliding on the now slushy ice that was beneath her shoes.

"Come inside. We're going to catch frostbite."

The storm began to rage on, and she just stood there, staring at me.

"How could you think so little of yourself? How could you think I would think so little of you?"

"It wasn't just that. I know you didn't think that. But you could. There were so many opportunities for you.

Opportunities you took. But you were afraid to go on those trips because you didn't want to leave me behind. And I didn't want to be the person you resented."

"And you didn't let me have that choice. You took it all away because you thought I would resent you? I resent you now for leaving me. For breaking my heart. You broke me, August. I've never loved anyone else. Including the other man I married. Anyone else was always in comparison to you, and you thought you weren't good enough? What did you think of me if you thought I would even contemplate that?"

"I'm sorry. I know I'm wrong. I know I was wrong."

My voice broke as I spoke, and it had nothing to do with the freezing temperatures. Instead, she just stood there, shivering.

"What else? What did my mom do?"

"You don't need to hear that, Paisley."

"Fuck off. Tell me. I deserve to know. I've already cut my mother out of my life, something I should have done long ago. But what else did she do? Tell me, August Cassidy."

"She was constantly trying to marry you off. To those other businessmen? Like she did with Jacob?"

"And? I knew what she was doing. She had been trying since I was a teenager. It was disgusting."

"Well, do you remember the Jefferson Company?"

Paisley frowned, before her eyes widened. "The company that tried to buy me out. And then ended up stopping halfway. When another company came toward me. What does that have to do with it?"

"He was going to undercut you. Stop the business deals. Your mother and him had a scheme. You know your mom."

"A scheme," she whispered.

"They were going to take the business out from under you, deem you unfit, and sell it to the highest bidder. And if that didn't work, your mother had plans to undercut you at every contract that you had. She had been working for months. Because you wouldn't listen to her. Because you wouldn't leave me. And I couldn't let you lose your dream. So I walked away. So you could thrive."

I should have expected a punch, a slap, but I hadn't expected the full push. She shoved at my shoulders, and I slid down, only reaching out and taking her with me when I hadn't meant to. We both hit the ground, me taking the brunt of it, as she shouted.

"Are you kidding me, August Cassidy?"

"Stop full naming me," I snapped, as I tried to get up, both of us continuing to slide in the increasing snow around us.

"We need to get inside. We're going to catch hypothermia."

"Well, you deserve it. How could you think that any of that mattered to me?"

I stood up, barely keeping myself steady enough not to fall again, and then I was holding her tightly to me.

The wind was roaring, and I knew the blizzard was going to hit soon, but I just held her close.

"She was going to destroy your company."

"That I would've rebuilt. I would've found another way. Or you could have talked to me, so I was prepared. But you did nothing."

"Because I was afraid. Because you were so amazing and talented, and I was so stupid. And then my parents came to town, and they were drunk, and they were fighting and they were reminding me exactly why marriage never worked." I shook my head, and she just stared at me, tears streaming down her face.

"And I was wrong. I was so fucking wrong."

"You were. You are. You were selfish and you took our choices away from us. And then you tried to do it again. Did my mother help you this time?"

I shook my head as I pulled her toward the cabin, the snow coming down quickly. It was already accumulating, and I had a feeling that I would be using the generator sooner rather than later.

"We need to get inside. It's not safe."

"Fine. Only because I don't want to freeze out here when I'm still angry."

I held back a chuckle as we walked inside and shook off the snow. The power flickered once, then twice, and then it was just the fire in the fireplace keeping us lit.

The sun was still behind clouds, so it wasn't pitch black, but it was going to be soon.

"I need to work on the generator, and a few other things. To keep us safe overnight."

"I'll help. But first, were you ever going to talk to me again?"

I stared at her as the light from the fire flickered over her face, and we were silent for so long, that every emotion that she felt hit me hard.

Fear, agony, resignation, and acceptance.

Hell. I was such a damn idiot.

"I love you, Paisley."

Her eyes widened. "What?"

"I love you. I was up here trying to figure out how I was going to be a hermit so I would never have to see you again because it was too damn hard. Because I was such a coward for walking away all those years ago and again. If you want me to get down on my knees in the dirt and the snow and grovel, I will. But I should have fought for you. I just thought I was keeping you safe. And I realize now I was so wrong."

"Just like that. You want me to forgive you just like that."

"No, I want you to take your time to forgive me. Figure out if you still love me. Because walking away to protect you before might've been noble in some eyes, but it was such a fucking mistake that I've been trying to make up for it ever since. And at the wedding? I was scared. But I was going to try to find a way to fix it. Even if it took me far too long to realize how. Even if I'm still trying to figure out how."

As the power went back on again, and then turned back off, I saw Paisley's face drain of color before she wrapped her arms in my coat.

"I kept telling myself that falling in love with you would be a mistake. That wanting to be with you would be a mistake. And I will forever hate my mother for what she did, hate Jacob for the same. But I don't want to hate you anymore. I just want to figure out who we are. Without the labels, without the secrets. Without the fear that we'll become our parents. Just love me, August. And trust me. That's all I ask."

I slid my thumbs along her cheeks, wiping away her tears.

"I will love you until the end of our days, Paisley Cassidy Renee."

"Don't full name me," she teased. "But I love you. Even when it would've been easier for me not to, I loved you. Just help me trust you. That's all I ask."

"Every moment that we have together I will do my best so you can trust me again. Give me a second chance. A third chance. Give me all the chances. But let me be yours. I love you, Paisley. And I'm sorry for being scared. I'm sorry for walking away."

"And I'm sorry for not fighting when I needed to. I love you, August. So let's take that second chance. And let's see what happens. When it's just the two of us."

"No exes, no mothers, no parents, no drama. Just you and me."

"And no more running away."

And then my mouth was on hers, and the power went back on again, as the storm raged, and I held the woman that I loved close.

"You know, I only brought one sleeping bag. The beds aren't even made."

"Are you telling me that I'm going to have to cuddle with you in a sleeping bag next to a fire all night?" she asked.

"I know it'll be tough. But I'll find ways to keep you warm."

"You have so much groveling to do. So I guess you should probably start."

"So first the generator? And then I'll get on my knees."

She raised a brow. "Oh, you're going to be on your knees for a long while. Just saying. After all, I'm very bossy. Just ask anyone."

"Whatever you say, ma'am."

And as I kissed her again, and we laughed together, I knew that this was just one next step.

I had always loved her. Even when I told myself I couldn't. That I shouldn't.

And now I would spend the rest of my days promising her forever. And keeping that promise.

She was my first, my second, my always.

And it was about time that my heart, my soul, and my promises made that fact a forever. One second chance at a time.

Chapter Eighteen

Paisley

"**O**kay, are you ready for this?" Addison asked, as she worked on the train of my wedding dress.

My wedding dress.

As in, the dress I was wearing for my wedding.

My third wedding. Second to August.

There were already a few articles of that such, and I was a meme apparently in all the local circuits. But that was fine with me. They could all get their rocks off on my drama filled, soap opera wedding. Because in the end, I was about to marry the second chance husband of my lifetime, and the man who had groveled very well.

And not just in the way that others thought. In the way that he completely opened up with every single feeling he had. And was there for me.

There was no longer fear or worry about what would happen to us in the future. We were just it.

The first time around we had been young, impulsive, and scared to be hopeful.

Now we were a little bit older, maybe a little bit wiser, and far more scarred from our mistakes. But that's what we had learned.

We had both groveled for each other. And that was all that mattered.

"The dress is perfect, thank you, Devney, for finding it.

I looked toward one of my best friends and held up my hand. She slid hers into mine and squeezed. "I got lucky when I was shopping. And the fact that it was your size? Perfection."

It was a lovely lacy and flowy dress with an empire waist, and longer train than I would have thought possible to walk in. However, it worked for me. I felt like a fairytale princess, with flowers in my hair, and my long red tresses looking as if I had stepped out of a fairy book. And that's what we were going for.

We would be married by the cabin, a small ceremony with family and friends, near the place that we had finally torn open our souls and realized that happiness meant finding our truths by ourselves, and with each other.

There was nothing more that we needed.

"I think I'm going to cry." Devney wiped her tears, and I just grinned.

"Is it hormones or are you just happy?

My best friend put her hand over her swelling bump, and grinned. "Hormones."

"Well, I guess I'm right alongside both of you," Addison said with a grin, as she put her hand over her currently flat stomach. She was still in her first trimester, and ready for the next phase of her family.

I put my hand over my small bump and let out a breath.

"Well, three pregnant women and one wedding? There won't be any tears at all."

"I heard that Heath has stocked up on tissues for all of us, don't worry," Devney said with a laugh.

"I'm just happy that Greer is the sane one of all of us," I said as my future sister-in-law walked inside, bouquets in her hands.

"Seriously. Keeping up with your sets of hormones is a little ridiculous." She rolled her eyes and handed over the bouquets. "Are you guys ready?

"We are," Addison and Devney said at the same time.

As I sucked in a breath, knowing this was it. I stood

in a circle with the three women that were a major part of my life.

My mother was not part of my life. I had seen her twice since the fight in the office and hadn't seen her since. She seemed to have understood the lesson. I wouldn't have any contact with her again, and I was grateful. She knew about the wedding day, and that I was expecting. Because the rest of the world who followed our small little business sector knew. But she hadn't said a thing, and I didn't even feel an ounce of sadness that she hadn't contacted me. I hadn't heard from Jacob since threatening him with a restraining order. And last I had heard, he was now married to Lydia. Their broken relationship was back on, and they seemed happy. That was fine with me, and they would be a nice family together, far away from me. Our lives were no longer entwined in the media, or in truth. And that was one mistake I wouldn't have to make again.

But now I was coming home to the man I had been ready for all these years.

"I love you all. Thank you for being my family. Thank you for always being my *sisters*."

"And here we go," Addison said as tears streamed down her face, and Devney hiccupped a sob. Greer rolled her eyes and handed over handkerchiefs.

"Be strong, ladies. It's the happiest day."

"So happy!" Devney continued to sob.

"I love you all. Thank you for being my sisters. And I can't wait to get out there."

"Then let's do it," Greer said with a clap of her hands, and as we all cheered and walked outside the small cabin to where the setup for the wedding would be, I was ready.

My team was here, all of them bringing dates, and looking quite festive in their spring attire. Ace and Grace from Heath's bar were there, looking quite happy with the baby in their arms. Noah and Ford were there as well, the lead ushers to keep the family organized. All of Devney's family were there, including her multiple siblings, step-siblings, her parents, and all of the next generation. It was quite astonishing how many of Devney's family were out there.

Luca's partner from the vet clinic was there, as well as Addison's friends from college. A few other people that we had met along the way, including some local friends that we had found during our dating and courting.

A few teachers from August's school were there, including Dakota. I grinned at her and she leaned into her wife and gave me a little wave.

Everybody just looked so happy and ready for this.

Julia and Gerald Cassidy, the infamous parents were there as well, still married, and quiet as they watched our wedding unfold. I didn't know what August had said to threaten them, or maybe it had been Heath and Luca. Maybe even Greer. I wasn't sure, but all that mattered was the man at the end of the aisle. Luca and Heath were there as well, waiting for their wives to meet them down the aisle.

Greer stood at the center of it all, the one who would marry us. She hadn't wanted to make the choice of whose side to stand on, so she would be officiating the nuptials.

August holding his baby sister as he asked her would always be a memory for me. The way they'd both cried and I'd sobbed right along with the two of them.

Greer's husbands sat next to each other on my side of the aisle in place of my parents, and I was grateful for that. They were my family now after all.

And as I stood at the end of the aisle, and waited for the violin to begin, I looked at the man who had once been my husband, and would be my husband again, and smiled.

I hadn't even realized I was moving until people were standing, and laughing, because I was ahead of the music, but it didn't matter. I just needed to get to the love of my life.

"Impatient, are we?" he asked, as he wrapped his arms around my waist. I put my hands on his cheeks and went to my tiptoes.

"Kiss me?"

"As you wish." And then his lips were on mine, and I was sighing into him, and people were laughing and whistling.

"Get a room!" someone called, and Devney shushed them. It must have been one of her siblings.

But I just smiled up at my first husband, and soon to be my third.

"Are you ready for this?"

"I've been waiting for always. It isn't every day that you get to marry your ex-wife."

"I mean, former ex-husband turned current husband does have a nice ring to it."

"Practically rolls off the tongue."

People continued to laugh, and then I held my husband's hands, as August put his over my stomach as our babies, both of them, kicked his palms.

Joy, such joy filled his gaze, as we vowed to each other that we would be honest, open, and for one another.

I had signed my name on a dotted line all those years ago, not realizing the truth that came from those vows. I could sign my name and all legal ties day in and day out, but they wouldn't matter as much as the signature I inscribed today.

I was a title, I was a promise, and I was now a wife. Again.

It had taken me far too long to realize who I could be. Who I needed to be. And in the end, signing my name wasn't signing away my future, or my past. It was signing a promise.

It was signing a second chance I hadn't seen coming.

And as my new husband kissed me, and our babies kicked, I knew this promise was just the beginning of a forever.

One vow at a time.

Get caught up in the next series from Carrie Ann Ryan, featuring Ford Cage's family! The Forever Rule (The Cage Family Book 1)

IF YOU'D LIKE TO READ A BONUS SCENE FROM
PAISLEY & AUGUST:
CHECK OUT THIS SPECIAL EPILOGUE!

If you'd like to read the next Generation with the Montgomery Ink Legacy Series: Bittersweet Promises

In the mood for more small town romance? Check out the Ashford Creek series with LEGACY. Or as I like to call it "The Small Town of Single Dads".

A Note from Carrie Ann Ryan

Thank you so much for reading **SECOND CHANCE HUSBAND.**

I love second chance stories where figuring out who you are NOW can totally change how you saw yourself THEN. August and Paisley deserved each other—even if it took them far too long to see the truth.

I truly hope you loved this series and I'm so happy you came along for the ride!

And if you'd like to read about Greer's story with her two men, you can read it in Best Friend Temptation!

The Falling for the Cassidy Brothers Series:

Get caught up in the next series from Carrie Ann Ryan, featuring Ford Cage's family! The Forever Rule (The Cage Family Book 1)

IF YOU'D LIKE TO READ A BONUS SCENE FROM
PAISLEY & AUGUST:
CHECK OUT THIS SPECIAL EPILOGUE!

If you want to make sure you know what's coming next from me, you can sign up for my newsletter at www. CarrieAnnRyan.com; follow me on twitter at @CarrieAnnRyan, or like my Facebook page. I also have a Facebook Fan Club where we have trivia, chats, and other goodies. You guys are the reason I get to do what I do and I thank you.

Make sure you're signed up for my MAILING LIST so you can know when the next releases are available as well as find giveaways and FREE READS.

Happy Reading!

Also from Carrie Ann Ryan

The Montgomery Ink Legacy Series:

Book 1: Bittersweet Promises (Leif & Brooke)

Book 2: At First Meet (Nick & Lake)

Book 2.5: Happily Ever Never (May & Leo)

Book 3: Longtime Crush (Sebastian & Raven)

Book 4: Best Friend Temptation (Noah, Ford, and Greer)

Book 4.5: Happily Ever Maybe (Jennifer & Gus)

Book 5: Last First Kiss (Daisy & Hugh)

Book 6: His Second Chance (Kane & Phoebe)

Book 7: One Night with You (Kingston & Claire)

Book 8: Accidentally Forever (Crew & Aria)

Book 9: Last Chance Seduction (Lexington & Mercy)

Book 10: Kiss Me Forever (Brooklyn & Reece)

Carrie Ann Ryan

Book 11: His Guilty Pleasure (Dash & Aly)

Book 12: Maybe it's You (Riley & Gage)

The Cage Family

Book 1: The Forever Rule (Aston & Blakely)

Book 2: An Unexpected Everything (Isabella & Weston)

Book 3: If You Were Mine (Dorian & Harper)

Book 4: One Quick Obsession (Hudson & Scarlett)

Book 5: Pretend it's Forever (Sophia & Carson)

Book 6: Wish it Were You (Flynn & Luna)

Ashford Creek

Book 1: Legacy (Callum & Felicity)

Book 2: Crossroads (Bodhi & Kiera)

Book 3: Westward (Atlas & Elizabeth)

Book 4: Patience (Teagan & Rush)

Clover Lake

Book 1: Always a Fake Bridesmaid (Livvy & Ewan)

Book 2: Accidental Runaway Groom (Jamie & Sharp)

Book 3: His Practically Fake Proposal (Galen & Addy)

The Wilder Brothers Series:

Book 1: One Way Back to Me (Eli & Alexis)

Book 2: Always the One for Me (Evan & Kendall)

Book 3: The Path to You (Everett & Bethany)

Book 4: Coming Home for Us (Elijah & Maddie)

Book 5: Stay Here With Me (East & Lark)

Book 6: Finding the Road to Us (Elliot, Trace, and Sidney)

Book 7: Moments for You (Ridge & Aurora)

Book 7.5: A Wilder Wedding (Amos & Naomi)

Book 8: Forever For Us (Wyatt & Ava)

Book 9: Pieces of Me (Gabriel & Briar)

Book 10: Endlessly Yours (Brooks & Rory)

The Falling for the Cassidy Brothers Series:

(Formerly the First Time Series)

Book 1: Good Time Boyfriend (Heath & Devney)

Book 2: Last Minute Fiancé (Luca & Addison)

Book 3: Second Chance Husband (August & Paisley)

Montgomery Ink Denver:

Book 0.5: Ink Inspired (Shep & Shea)

Book 0.6: Ink Reunited (Sassy, Rare, and Ian)

Book 1: Delicate Ink (Austin & Sierra)

Book 1.5: Forever Ink (Callie & Morgan)

Montgomery Ink: Colorado Springs

The Montgomery Ink: Boulder Series:

Book 1: Wrapped in Ink (Liam & Arden)

Book 2: Sated in Ink (Ethan, Lincoln, and Holland)

Book 3: Embraced in Ink (Bristol & Marcus)

Book 3: Moments in Ink (Zia & Meredith)

Book 4: Seduced in Ink (Aaron & Madison)

Book 4.5: Captured in Ink (Julia, Ronin, & Kincaid)

Book 4.7: Inked Fantasy (Secret ??)

Book 4.8: A Very Montgomery Christmas (The Entire Boulder Family)

The Montgomery Ink: Fort Collins Series:

Book 1: Inked Persuasion (Jacob & Annabelle)

Book 2: Inked Obsession (Beckett & Eliza)

Book 3: Inked Devotion (Benjamin & Brenna)

Book 3.5: Nothing But Ink (Clay & Riggs)

Book 4: Inked Craving (Lee & Paige)

Book 5: Inked Temptation (Archer & Killian)

The Promise Me Series:

Book 1: Forever Only Once (Cross & Hazel)

Book 2: From That Moment (Prior & Paris)

Book 3: Far From Destined (Macon & Dakota)

Book 4: From Our First (Nate & Myra)

The Whiskey and Lies Series:

Book 1: <u>Whiskey Secrets</u> (Dare & Kenzie)

Book 2: <u>Whiskey Reveals</u> (Fox & Melody)

Book 3: <u>Whiskey Undone</u> (Loch & Ainsley)

The Gallagher Brothers Series:

Book 1: <u>Love Restored</u> (Graham & Blake)

Book 2: <u>Passion Restored</u> (Owen & Liz)

Book 3: <u>Hope Restored</u> (Murphy & Tessa)

The Carr Family Series:

(Formerly the Less Than Series)

Book 1: Breathless With Her (Devin & Erin)

Book 2: Reckless With You (Tucker & Amelia)

Book 3: Shameless With Him (Caleb & Zoey)

The Fractured Connections Series:

Book 1: Breaking Without You (Cameron & Violet)

Book 2: Shouldn't Have You (Brendon & Harmony)

Book 3: Falling With You (Aiden & Sienna)

Book 4: Taken With You (Beckham & Meadow)

The Campus Roommates Series:

(Formerly the On My Own Series)

Book 0.5: My First Glance

Book 1: My One Night (Dillon & Elise)

Book 2: My Rebound (Pacey & Mackenzie)

Book 3: My Next Play (Miles & Nessa)

Book 4: My Bad Decisions (Tanner & Natalie)

The Ravenwood Coven Series:

Book 1: Dawn Unearthed

Book 2: Dusk Unveiled

Book 3: Evernight Unleashed

The Aspen Pack Series:

Book 1: Etched in Honor

Book 2: Hunted in Darkness

Book 3: Mated in Chaos

Book 4: Harbored in Silence

Book 5: Marked in Flames

The Talon Pack:

Book 1: Tattered Loyalties

Book 2: An Alpha's Choice

Book 3: Mated in Mist

Book 4: Wolf Betrayed

Book 5: Fractured Silence

Book 6: Destiny Disgraced

Book 7: Eternal Mourning

Book 8: Strength Enduring

Book 9: Forever Broken

Book 10: Mated in Darkness

Carrie Ann Ryan

Book 2: <u>Her Warriors' Three Wishes</u>

Book 3: <u>An Unlucky Moon</u>

Book 3.5: <u>His Choice</u>

Book 4: <u>Tangled Innocence</u>

Book 5: <u>Fierce Enchantment</u>

Book 6: <u>An Immortal's Song</u>

Book 7: <u>Prowled Darkness</u>

Book 8: Dante's Circle Reborn

Holiday, Montana Series:

Book 1: <u>Charmed Spirits</u>

Book 2: <u>Santa's Executive</u>

Book 3: <u>Finding Abigail</u>

Book 4: <u>Her Lucky Love</u>

Book 5: Dreams of Ivory

The Branded Pack Series:
(Written with Alexandra Ivy)

Book 1: <u>Stolen and Forgiven</u>

Book 2: <u>Abandoned and Unseen</u>

Book 3: <u>Buried and Shadowed</u>

From The Forever Rule

Aston

*The Cages are the most prestigious family in Denver—at least according to the patriarch of the Cage Family.
And the Cages have rules.
Rules only they know.*

I always knew that one day my father would die. I hadn't realized that day would come so soon. Or that the last words I would say to him would've been in anger.

I had been having one of the best nights of my life, a beautiful woman in my arms, and a smile on my face when I received the phone call that had changed my family's life.

The fact that I had been smiling had been a shock, because according to my brothers, I didn't smile much. I was far too busy being *The Cage* of Cage Enterprises.

We were a dominant force in the city of Denver when it came to certain real estate ventures, as well as being one of the only ethical and environmentally friendly ones who tried to keep up with that. We had our hands in countless different pots around the world, but mostly we gravitated in the state of Colorado—our home.

I had not created the company, no, that honor had gone to my grandfather, and then my father. The Cage Enterprises were and would always be a family endeavor. And when my father had stepped away a few years ago, stating he had wanted to see the world, and also see if his sons could actually take up the mantle, I had stepped in—not that the man believed we could.

My brothers were in various roles within the company, at least those who had wanted to be part of it. But I was the face of Cage Enterprises.

So no, I hadn't smiled often. There wasn't time. We weren't billionaires with mega yachts. We worked seventy-hour weeks to make sure *all* our employees had a livable wage while wining and dining with those who looked down at us for not being on their level. And others thought we were the high and mighty anyway since they didn't understand us. So, I didn't smile.

But I had smiled that night.

It had been a gala for some charity, one I couldn't even remember off the top of my head. We had donated between the company and my own finances—we always did. But I couldn't even remember anything about why we were there.

Yet I could remember her smile. The heat in her eyes when she had looked up at me, the feel of her body pressed against mine as we had danced along the dance floor, and then when we ended up in the hallway, bodies pressed against one another, needing each other, wanting each other.

And I had put aside all my usual concepts of business and life to have this woman in my arms.

And then my mother had called and had shattered that illusion.

"Your father is dead."

She hadn't even braced me for the blow. A heart attack on a vacation on a beach in Majorca, and he was dead. She hadn't cried, hadn't said anything, just told me that I had to be the one to tell my brothers.

And so, I had, all six of them. Because of course Loren Cage would have seven sons. He couldn't do things just once, he had to make sure he left his legacy, his destiny.

And that was why we were here today, in a high-rise in Centennial, waiting on my father's lawyer to show up with the reading of the will.

"Hey, when is Winstone going to get here?" Dorian asked, his typical high energy playing on his face, and how he tapped his fingers along the hand-carved wooden table.

I stared at my brother, at those piercing blue eyes that matched my own, and frowned. He should be here soon. He did call us all here after all."

"I still don't know why we all had to be here for the reading of the will," Hudson whispered as he stared off into the distance. Neither Dorian nor Hudson worked for Cage Enterprises. They had stock with the company, and a few other connections because that's what family did, but they didn't work on the same floors as some of us and hadn't been elbow to elbow with our father before he had retired. Though dear old dad had worked in our small town more often than not in the end. In fact, Hudson didn't even live in Denver anymore. He had moved to the town we owned in the mountains.

Because of course we Cages owned a damned town. Part of me wasn't sure if the concept of having our name on everything within the town had been on purpose or had occurred organically. Though knowing my grandfather, perhaps it had been exactly what he'd wanted. He had bought up a few buildings, built a few more, and now we owned three-quarters of the town, including the major resort which brought in tourists and income.

And that was why we were here.

"You have to be here because you're evidently in the will," I said softly, trying not to get annoyed that we were waiting for our father's lawyer. Again.

"You would think he would be able to just send us a memo. I mean, it should be clear right? We all know what stakes we have in, we should just be able to do things evenly," Theo said, his gaze off into the distance. My younger brother also didn't work for the company, instead he had decided to go to culinary school, something my father had hated. But you couldn't control a Cage, that was sort of our deal.

"Why would you be cut out of the will?" I asked, honestly curious.

"Because I married a man and a woman," he drawled out. "You know he hasn't spoken to me since before the wedding," Ford said, and I saw the hurt in his gaze even though I knew he was probably trying to hide it.

"Well, he was an asshole, what do you expect?" James asked.

I looked behind Ford to see my brother and co-chair of Cage Enterprises standing with his hands in his pockets, staring out the window.

With Flynn, our vice president, standing beside him, they looked like the heads of businesses they were. While they wore suits and so did I, we were the only ones.

Dorian and Hudson were both in jeans, Hudson's having a hole at the knee. And probably not as a fashion statement, most likely because it had torn at some point, and he hadn't bothered to buy another pair. Theo was in slacks, but a Henley with his sleeves pushed up, tapping his finger just like Hudson, clearly wanting to get out of here as well. Ford had on cargo pants, and a tight black T-shirt, and looked like he had just gotten off his shift. He owned a security company with his husband and a few other friends, and did security for the Cages when he could, though I knew he didn't like to work with family often. And I knew it wasn't because of us. No, it was Father—even if he had officially *retired*. It was always Father.

And he was gone.

"Can't believe the asshole's gone," I whispered.

Ford's brows rose. "Look at that, you calling him an asshole. I'm proud."

"You should show him respect," Mother said as she

came inside the room, her high heels tapping against the marble floors. I didn't bother standing up like I normally would have, because Melanie Cage looked to be in a *mood*.

She didn't look sad that Dad was gone, more like angry that he would dare go against their plans. What plans? I didn't know, but that was my mother.

She came right up to Dorian and leaned down to kiss his cheek. She didn't even bother to look at the rest of us. Dorian was Mother's favorite. Which I knew Dorian resented, but I didn't have to deal with mommy issues at this moment.

No, we had to deal with father issues at this point.

"I'm going to go get him," Flynn replied, turning toward the door. "I'm really not in the mood to wait any longer, especially since he's being so secretive about this meeting."

As I had been thinking just the same, I nodded at Flynn though he didn't need my permission. However, just then, the door opened, and I frowned when it wasn't just Mr. Winstone walking into the conference room.

I stared as an older woman walked through the door following Mr. Winstone, and four women and another man with messy hair and tattered cut-up jeans that matched Hudson's walked behind them.

The guy looked familiar, as if I'd seen him somewhere, or maybe it was just his eyes.

Where had I seen those eyes before?

"Phoebe? What are you doing here?" Ford asked as he moved forward and gripped the hands of one of the women.

"I was going to ask the same question," Phoebe asked as she looked at Ford, then around the room.

Those of us sitting stood up, confused about why this other family—because they were clearly a family—had decided to enter the room.

"We're here to meet the lawyer about my father's death, Ford. Why would you and the Cages be here?" she asked, and I wondered how the hell Mr. Winstone had fucked up so badly? Why the hell was he letting another family that clearly seemed to be in shock come into our room? This wasn't how he normally handled things.

Ford was the one who answered though—thankfully —because I had no idea what the hell was going on.

"Phoebe, we're here for my dad's will reading. What the hell is going on?" he asked. Phoebe looked around, as well as the others.

I stared at them, at the tall willowy one with wide eyes, at the smaller one with tears still in her eyes as if she was the only one truly mourning, and at the woman who seemed to be in charge, not the mother. Instead she had shrewd eyes and was glaring at all of us. The man stood back, hands in pockets, and looked just as shell-shocked as Ford.

But before Mr. Winstone or anyone else could say anything, my mother spoke in such a crisp, icy tone that I froze.

"I don't know why you're acting so dramatic. You knew your father was an asshole. He just liked creating drama," she snapped.

As I tried to catch up with her words, the older woman answered. "Melanie, stop."

This couldn't be happening. Because things started to click into place. The fact that the man at the other end of this table had our eyes, and that everybody looked so fucking shocked. I didn't know how Ford knew this Phoebe, and I would be getting answers.

"We had a deal," my mother continued, as it seemed that the rest of us were just now catching on. "You would keep your family away from mine. We would share Loren, but I got the name, I got the family. You got whatever else. But now it looks like Loren decided to be an asshole again."

"What are you talking about?" the shrewd sister asked as she came forward, her hands fisted at her side.

"Excuse me," I said, clearing my throat. I was going to be damned if I let anyone else handle this meeting. I was The Cage now. "Will someone please explain?"

"Well, I wasn't quite sure how this was going to work out," Mr. Winstone began, and we all quieted, while I wanted to strangle the man. What did he mean how *the hell this would work out*? What was this?

This seemed like a big fucking mistake.

"Loren Cage had certain provisions in his will for both of his families. And one of the many requirements that I will go over today is that this meeting must take place." He paused and I hoped it wasn't for effect, because I was going to throttle him if it was. "Loren Cage had two families. Seven sons with his wife Melanie, and four daughters and a son with his mistress, Constance."

"We went by partner," the other mother corrected.

I blinked, counting the adults in the room. "Twelve?" I asked, my voice slightly high-pitched.

"Busy fucking man," Dorian whispered.

Hudson snorted, while we just stood and stared at each other.

This could not be happening. A secret family? No, we were not that cliché.

"I can't do this," Phoebe blurted, her eyes wide.

"Oh, stop overreacting," my mother scorned.

"Do not talk to my daughter that way." The other mother glared.

"It was always going to be an issue," Mother continued. "All the secrets and the lies. And now the kids will have to deal with it. Because God forbid Loren ever deal with anything other than his own dick."

"That's enough," I snapped.

"Don't you dare talk to us like that," the shrewd sister snapped right back.

"I will talk however I damn well please. I am going to need to know exactly how this happened," I shouted over everyone else's words.

Out of the corner of my eye I saw Phoebe run through the door. Ford followed and then the tall willowy one joined.

"Shit," I snapped.

"Language," Mother bit out.

I laughed. "Really? You are going to talk to me about language."

I looked over at James, who shrugged, before he put two fingers in his mouth and whistled that high-pitched whistle that only he could do.

Everyone froze as Theo rubbed his ear and glared at me.

"Winstone," I said through gritted teeth. "I take it we all have to be here in order for this to happen?"

He cleared his throat. "At least a majority. But you all had to at least step into the room."

"Excuse me then," I said.

"You're just going to leave? Just like that?" my mother asked.

I whirled on her. "I'm going to go see if my apparent *family* is okay. Then I'm going to come back and we're going to get answers. Because there is no way that I'm going to leave here without them."

I stormed out the door, and thankfully nobody followed me.

Of course, though, I shouldn't have been too swift with that, as the woman who had to be the eldest sister practically ran to my side, her heels tapping against the marble.

"I'm coming with you."

"That's just fine." I paused, knowing that I wasn't angry at these people. No, my father and apparently our mothers were the ones that had to deal with this. I looked over at the woman who Mr. Winstone and the mothers had claimed was my sister and cleared my throat.

"I'm Aston."

"Is this really the time for introductions?" she asked.

"I'm about to go see your sister and my brother to make sure that they're fine, so sure. I would like to know the name of the woman that is running next to me right now."

"I'm running, you're walking quickly because you have such long legs."

I snorted, surprised I could even do that.

"I'm Isabella," she replied after a moment.

"I would say nice to meet you Isabella..." I let my voice trail off.

She let out a sharp laugh before shaking her head. "I'm going to need a moment to wrap my head around this, but not now."

"Same."

We stormed out of the building, and I lagged behind since Ford was standing in front of Phoebe who was in the arms of another man with dark hair and everybody seemed to be talking all at once.

"I just. I can't deal with this right now," Phoebe said, and I realized that something else must have been going on with her right then. She looked tired, and far more emotional than the rest of us.

I looked over at the man holding her and blinked. "Kane?" I asked.

Kane stared at me and let out a breath. "Wow," he said with a laugh.

"We'll handle it," Isabella put in, completely ignoring us. "And if we need to meet again later, we will." Then she looked over at Ford and I, with such menace in her gaze, I nearly took a step back. "Is that a problem?"

I raised my chin, glaring right back at her. "Not at all. However I want answers, so I'd rather not have the meeting canceled right now. But I'm also not going to force any of my," I paused, realization hitting far too hard, "*family* to stay if they don't want to."

And with that, I turned on my heel and went back into the building, with Isabella and Ford following me. Everyone was still yelling in the interim, and I cleared my throat. As Isabella had done it at the same time, everyone paused to look at me.

"Read the damn will. Because we need answers," I ordered Winstone, and he shook like a leaf before nodding.

"Okay. We can do that." He cleared his throat, then he began going over trusts and incomes and buildings and things that I would care about soon, but what I wanted to know was what the hell our father had been thinking about.

"Here's the tricky part," Winstone began, as we all leaned forward, eager to hear what the hell he had to say.

"The family money, not of the business, not of each of your inheritance from other family members, but the bulk of Loren Cage's assets will be split between all twelve kids."

"Are you kidding me?" Isabella asked. "What money? We weren't exactly poor, but we were solidly middle class."

"We did just fine," the other mother pleaded.

My mother snorted, clearly not believing the words.

I glared at the woman who raised me, willing her to say *anything*. She would probably be pushed out of the window at that point. Not by me, by someone else, but she probably would've earned it.

The lawyer continued. "However to retain the majority of current assets and to keep Cage Lake and all of its subsidiaries you will have to meet as a family once a month for three years. If this does not happen, Cage Enterprises will be broken into multiple parts and sold." He went on into the legalese that I ignored as I tried to hear over the blood pounding in my ears.

"You own a town?" the other man asked.

I looked over at the one man in the room I didn't know the name of. "Not exactly."

"Kyler," Isabella whispered.

In that moment, I realized that I had a brother named Kyler—if this was all to be believed.

"This can't be legal right?" the tall willowy person said.

"Yes Sophia, it can," their mother put in.

Oh good, another sister named Sophia.

Only one name to go. What the hell was wrong with me?

I forced my jaw to relax. "Are you telling us that we need to have all twelve of us at dinner once a month for three years in order to keep what is rightly inherited to us? To keep people in business and keep their jobs?"

"We don't need the money, but everyone else in our employ does," James snapped. "As do those we work with."

"Damn straight," Dorian growled.

"How are we supposed to believe this?" I asked, asking the obvious question.

"First, only five must attend, and two must be of a different family." The lawyer continued as if I hadn't spoken. "Of course you are *all* family..."

"Again, how are we supposed to believe this?" I asked.

"Here are the DNA tests already done."

"Are you fucking kidding me?" Isabella asked.

I looked at her, as she had literally taken the words out of my mouth.

"Isn't that sort of like a violation?" Kyler asked, his face pale.

"We need to get our own lawyers on this," James whispered.

I nodded tightly, knowing we had much more to say on this.

"There's no way this is legal," the youngest said, and I looked over at her.

"What's your name?" I asked.

"Emily. Emily Cage Dixon," she said softly, and we all froze.

"Your middle name is Cage?" I asked, biting out the words.

"All of our middle names are Cage," Sophia said, shaking her head. "I hated it but Dad wanted to be cute because our father's name was Cage Dixon, or maybe it wasn't. Is he also a bigamist?" she asked.

Her mother lifted her chin. "We never married. And no, your father's name was not Dixon, that was my maiden name."

"What?" Sophia asked. "All this time...are our grandparents even dead?"

"Yes, my parents are dead. The same with Loren's."

The other mother's eyes filled with tears. "I'm sorry we lied."

"We'll get to that later," Isabella put in, and I was grateful.

I let out a breath. "In order to keep our assets, in order to keep the family name intact, we need to have *dinner*. For three years."

The small lawyer nodded, his glasses falling down his nose. "At least five of you. And it can start three months after the funeral, which we can plan after this."

"This is ridiculous," Hudson murmured under his breath, before he got up and walked out.

I watched him go, knowing he had his own demons, and tried to understand what the hell was going on. "Why did he do this?" I asked, more to myself than anyone else.

"I never really knew the man, but apparently none of us did," Isabella said, staring off into the distance.

"Leave the paperwork and go," I ordered Winstone, and he didn't even mutter a peep. Instead, he practically ran out of the room. James and Flynn immediately went to the paperwork, and I knew they were scouring it. But from the way that their jaws tightened, I had a feeling that my father had found a way to make this legal. Because we would always have a choice to lose everything. That was the man.

"It's true," my mother put in. "You all share the same father. That was the deal when we got married, and when he decided to bring this other woman into our lives."

"I'm pretty sure you were the other woman," the other mom said.

I pinched the bridge of my nose.

"Stop. All of you." I stared at the group and realized that I was probably the eldest Cage here, other than the moms. I would deal with this. We didn't have a choice. "Whatever happens, we'll deal with it."

"You're in charge now?" Isabella asked, but Sophia shushed her.

I was grateful for that, because I had a feeling Isabella and I were going to butt heads more often than not.

I shrugged, trying to act as if my world hadn't been rocked. "I would say welcome to the Cages, because DNA evidence seems to point that way, however perhaps you were already one of us all along."

Kyler muttered something under his breath I couldn't hear before speaking up. "You have my eyes," he said.

I nodded. "Noticed that too."

The other man tilted his head. "So what, we do dinners and we make nice?"

I sighed. "We don't have to be adversaries."

"You say that as if you're the one in charge," Isabella said again.

"Because he is," Theo said, and they all stared at him.

I tried to tamp down the pride swelling at those words—along with the overwhelming pressure.

Theo continued. "He's the eldest. He's the one that takes care of us. And he's the CEO of Cage Enterprises. He's going to be the one that deals with the paperwork fallout."

"Because family is just paperwork?" Emily asked, her voice lost.

I shook my head. "No, family is insane, and apparently, it's been secret all along. And it looks like we have a few introductions to make, and a few tests to redo. But if it turns out it's true, we're Cages, and we don't back down."

"And what does that mean?" Isabella asked, her tone far too careful.

Theo was the one who finally answered. "It means we're going to have to figure shit out."

And for just an instant, the thought of that beautiful woman with that gorgeous smile came to mind, and I pushed those thoughts away. My family was breaking, or perhaps breaking open. And I didn't have time to worry about things like a woman who had made me smile.

The Cages needed me and after today's meeting there would be no going back to sanity.

Ever.

In the mood to read another family saga?
Meet the Cage Family in The Forever Rule!

From One Way Back to Me

Eli

When my morning begins with me standing ankle-deep in a basement full of water, I know I probably should have stayed in bed. Only, I was the boss, and I didn't get that choice.

"Hold on. I'm looking for it." East cursed underneath his breath as my younger brother bent down around the pipe, trying his best to turn off the valve. I sighed, waded through the muck in my work boots, and moved to help him. "I said I've got it," East snapped, but I ignored him.

I narrowed my eyes at the evil pipe. "It's old and rusted, and even though it passed an inspection over a year ago, we knew this was going to be a problem."

"And I'm the fucking handyman of this company. I've got this."

"And as a handyman, you need a hand."

"You're hilarious. Seriously. I don't know how I could ever manage without your wit and humor." The dryness in his tone made my lips twitch even as I did my best to ignore the smell of whatever water we stood in.

"Fuck you," I growled.

"No thanks. I'm a little too busy for that."

With a grunt, East shut off the water, and we both stood back, hands on our hips as we stared at the mess of this basement.

East let out a sigh. "I'm not going to have to turn the water off for the whole property, but I'm glad that we don't have tenants in this particular cabin."

I nodded tightly and held back a sigh. "This is probably why there aren't basements in Texas. Because everything seems to go wrong in these things."

"I'm pretty sure this is a storm shelter, or at least a tornado one. Not quite sure as it's one of the only basements in the area."

"It was probably the only one that they had the energy to make back in the day. Considering this whole place is built over clay and limestone."

East nodded, looked around. "I'll start the cleanup

with this water, and we'll look to see what we can do with the pipes."

I pinched the bridge of my nose. "I don't want to have to replace the plumbing for this whole place."

"At least it's not the villa itself, or the farmhouse, or the winery. Just a single cabin."

I glared at my younger brother, then reached out and knocked on a wooden pillar. "Shut your mouth. Don't say things like that to me. We are just now getting our feet under us."

East shrugged. "It's the truth, though. However much you weigh it, it could have been worse."

I pinched the bridge of my nose. "Jesus Christ. You were in the military for how long? A Wilder your entire life, and you say things like that? When the hell did you lose that superstition bone?"

"About the time that my Humvee was blown up, and when Evan's was, Everett's too. Hell, about the time that you almost fell out of the sky in your plane. Or when Elliot was nearly shot to death trying to help one of his men. So, yes, I pretty much lost all superstition when trying to toe the line ended up in near death and maiming."

I met my brother's gaze, that familiar pang thinking about all that we had lost and almost lost over the past few years.

East muttered under his breath, shaking his head. "And I sound more and more like Evan these days rather than myself."

I squeezed his shoulder and let out a breath, thinking of our brother who grunted more than spoke these days. "It's okay. We've been through a lot. But we're here."

Somehow, we were here. I wasn't quite sure if we had made the right decision about two years ago when we had formed this plan, or rather I had formed this plan, but there was no going back. We were in it, and we were going to have to find a way to make it work, flooded former tornado shelters and all.

East sighed. "I'll work on this now. Then I'll head on over to the main house. I have a few things to work on there."

"You know, we can hire you help. I know we had all the contractors and everything to work with us for some of the rebuilds and rehabs, but we can hire someone else for you on a day-to-day basis."

My brother shook his head. "We may be able to afford it, but I'd rather save that for a rainy day. Because when it rains, it pours here, and flash flooding is a major threat in this part of Texas." He winked as he said it, mixing his metaphors, and I just shook my head.

"You just let me know if you need it."

"You're the CEO, brother of mine, not the CFO. That's Everett."

"True, but we did talk about it so we can work on it." I paused, thinking about what other expenses might show up. "And what do you need to do with the villa?"

The villa was the main house where most things happened on the property. It contained the lobby, library, and atrium. My apartment was also on the top floor, so I could be there for emergencies. Our innkeeper lived on the other side of the house, but I was in the main loft because this was my project, my baby.

My other brothers, all five of them, lived in cabins on the property. We lived together, worked together, ate together, and fought together. We were the Wilder brothers. It was what we did.

I had left to join the Air Force at seventeen, having graduated early, leaving behind my kid brothers and sister. After nearly twenty years of doing what we needed to in order to survive, we hadn't spent as much time with one another as I would have liked. We hadn't been stationed together, so we hadn't seen one another for longer than holidays or in passing.

But now we were together. At least most of us. So I was going to make this work, even if it killed me.

East finally answered my question. "I just have to fix

a door that's a little too squeaky in one of the guestrooms. Not a big deal."

I raised a brow. "That's it?"

"It's one of the many things on my list. Thankfully, this place is big enough that I always have something to do. It's an unending list. And that the winery has its own team to work on all of that shit, because I'm not in the mood to learn to deal with any of the complicated machinery that comes with that world."

I snorted. "Honestly, same. I'm glad there are people that know what the fuck they're doing when it comes to wine making so that didn't have to be the two of us."

I left my brother to this job, knowing he liked time on his own, just like the rest of us did, and went to dry my boots. I was working by myself for most of the day, in interviews and other "boss business," as Elliot called it, so I had to focus and get clean.

I wasn't in the mood to deal with interviews, but it was part of my job. We had to fill positions that hadn't been working out over the past year, some more than others.

Wilder Retreat was a place that hadn't been even a spark in my mind my entire life. No, I had been too busy being a career military man—getting in my twenty, moving up the ranks, and ending up as a Lieutenant Colonel before I got out. I had been a commander of a squadron, and yet, it felt like I didn't know how to command where I was now.

When my sister Eliza had lost her husband when he was on deployment, it had been the last domino to fall in the Wilder brothers' military career. I had been ready to get out with twenty years in, knowing I needed a career outside of being a Lieutenant Colonel. I wasn't even forty yet, and the term retirement was a misnomer, but that's what happened when it came to my former job.

East had been getting out around that time for reasons of his own, and then Evan had been forced to. I rubbed my hand over my chest, that familiar pain, remembering the phone call from one of Evan's commanders when Evan had been hurt.

I thought I'd lost my baby brother then, and we nearly had. Everett had gotten hurt too, and Elijah and Elliot had needed out for their own reasons. Losing our baby sister's husband had just pushed us forward.

Finding out that Eliza's husband had been a cheating asshole had just cemented the fact that we needed to spend more time together as a family so we could be there for one another.

In retrospect, it would have been nice if Eliza would have been able to come down to Texas with us, to our suburb outside of San Antonio. Only, she had fallen in love again, with a man with a big family and a good heart up in Fort Collins, Colorado. She was still up there and traveled down enough that we actually got to get to know our sister again.

It was weird to think that, after so many years of always seeing each other in passing or through video calls, most of us were here, opening up a business. And all because I had been losing my mind.

Wilder Retreat and Winery was a villa and wedding venue outside of San Antonio. We were in hill country, at least what passed for hill country in South Texas, and the place had been owned by a former Air Force General who had wanted to retire and sell the place, since his kid didn't want it.

It was a large spread that used to be a ranch back in the day, nearly one hundred acres that the original owners had taken from a working ranch, and instead of making it a dude ranch or something similar, like others did around here, they'd added a winery using local help. We were close enough to Fredericksburg that it made sense in terms of the soil and weather. They had been able to add on additions, so it wasn't just the winery. Someone could come for the day for a winery tour or even a retreat tour, but most people came for the weekend or for a whole week. There were cabins and a farmhouse where we held weddings, dances, or other events. We had some chickens and ducks that gave us eggs, and goats that seemed to have a mind of their own and provided milk for cheese. Then there was the main annex, which housed all the equipment for the retreat villa.

The winery had its own section of buildings, and it was far bigger than anything I would have ever thought that we could handle. But, between the six of us, we did.

And the only reason we could even afford it, because one didn't afford something like this on a military salary, even with a decent retirement plan, was because of our uncles.

Our uncles, Edward and Edmond Wilder, had owned Wilder Wines down in Napa, California, for years. They had done well for themselves, and when we had been kids, we had gone out to visit. Evan had been the one that had clung to it and had been interested in wine making before he had changed his mind and gone into the military like the rest of us.

That was why Evan was in charge of the winery itself now. Because he knew what he was doing, even if he'd growled and said he didn't. Either way though, the place was huge, had multiple working parts at all times, and we had a staff that needed us. But when the uncles had died, they had left the money from the sale of the winery to us in equal parts. Eliza had taken hers to invest for her future children, and the rest of us had pooled our money together to buy this place and make it ours. A lot of the staff from the old owner had stayed, but some had left as well. Because they didn't want new owners who had no idea what they were doing, or they just retired. Either way, we were over a year in and doing okay.

Except for two positions that made me want to groan.

I had an interview with who would be our third wedding planner since we started this. The main component of the retreat was to have an actual wedding venue. To be able to host parties, and not just wine tours. Elliot was our major event planner that helped with our yearly and seasonal minute details, but he didn't want anything to do with the actual weddings. That was a whole other skill set, and so we wanted a wedding planner. We had gone through two wedding planners now, and we needed to hire a third. The first one had lied on her résumé, had given references that were her friends who had lied and had even created websites that were all fabrication, all so she could get into the business. Which, I understood, getting into the business is one thing. However, lying was another. Plus, we needed someone with actual experience because we didn't have any ourselves. We were going out on a limb here with this whole retreat business, and it was all because I had the harebrained idea of getting our family to work together, get along, and get to know one another. I wanted us to have a future, to be our own bosses.

And it was so far over my head that I knew that if I didn't get reliable help, we were going to fail.

Later, I had a meeting with that potential wedding planner. But first, I had to see what the fuck that smell was coming from the main kitchen in the villa.

The second wedding planner we hired was a guy with great and *true* references, one who was good at his job but hated everything to do with my brothers and me. He had hated the idea of the retreat and how rustic it was, even though we were in fucking South Texas. Yes, the buildings look slightly European because that was the theme that the original owners had gone for. Still, the guy had hated us, hadn't listened to us, and had called us white trash before he had walked away, jumped into his convertible, and sped off down the road, leaving us without help. He had been rude to our guests, and now Elliot was the one having to plan weddings for the past three weeks. My brother was going to strangle me soon if we didn't hire someone. And this person was going to be our last hope. As soon as she showed up, that was.

I looked down on my watch and tried to plan the rest of my day. I had thirty minutes to figure out what the hell was going on in the kitchen, and then I had to go to the meeting.

I nodded at a few guests who were sipping wine and eating a cheese plate and then at our innkeeper, Naomi. Naomi's honey-brown hair was cut in an angled bob that lit her face, and she grinned at me.

"Hello there, Boss Man," she whispered. "You might need to go to the kitchen."

"Do I want to know?" I asked with a grumble.

"I'm not sure. But I am going to go check in our next guest, and then Elliott needs to meet with the Henderson couple."

"He'll be there." I didn't say that Elliot would rather chew off his own arm rather than deal with this, considering we had a family event coming in, one that Elliot was on target with planning. The wedding for next year was an important one, so we needed to work on it.

Naomi was a fantastic innkeeper, far more organized than any of us—and that was saying something since my brothers and I knew our way around schedules, to-do lists, and spreadsheets. Naomi was personable, smiled, and kept us on our toes.

Without her, I knew we wouldn't be able to do this. Hell, without Amos, our vineyard manager, I knew that Evan and Elijah wouldn't be able to handle the winery as they did. Naomi and Amos had come with the place when we had bought it, and I would be forever grateful that they had decided to stay on.

I gave Naomi another nod, then headed back to the kitchen and nearly walked right back out.

Tony stood there, a scowl on his face and his hands on his hips. "I don't understand what the fuck is wrong with this oven."

"What's going on?" I asked as Everett stood by Tony. Everett was my quiet brother with usually a small smile on his face, only right then it looked like he was ready to scream.

I didn't know why Everett was even there since he was part responsible for the financials side of the company and usually worked with Elliot these days. Maybe he had come to the kitchen after the smell of burning as I had after Naomi's prodding.

Tony threw his hands in the air. "What's going on? This stove is a piece of shit. All of it is a piece of shit. I'm tired of this rustic place. I thought I would be coming to a Michelin star restaurant. To be my own chef. Instead, I have to make English breakfasts and pancakes with bananas. I might as well be at a bed and breakfast."

I pinched the bridge of my nose. "We're an inn, not a bed and breakfast."

"But I serve breakfast. That's all I do these days.

That and cheese platters. Nobody comes for dinner. Nobody comes for lunch."

That was a lie. Tony worked for the winery and the retreat itself and served all the meals. But Tony wanted to go crazy with the menu, to try new and fantastical items that just weren't going to work here.

And I had a feeling I was going to throw up if I wasn't careful.

"I quit," Tony snapped, and I knew right then, it was done for. I was done.

"You can't quit," I growled while Everett held back a sigh.

"Yes, I can. I'm done. I'm done with you and this ranch. You're not cowboys. You're not even Texans. You're just people moving in on our territory." And with that, Tony stomped away, throwing his chef's apron on the ground.

I was thankful that the kitchen was on the other side of the library and front area, where most of the guests were if they weren't out on one of the tours of the area and city that Elliott had arranged for them. That was the whole point of this retreat. They could come visit, and could relax, or we could set them up on a tour of downtown San Antonio, or Canyon Lake, or any of the other places that were nearby.

And yet, Tony had just thrown a wrench into all of

that. I didn't know what was worse, the smell of burning, Tony leaving, the water in the basement that wasn't truly a basement, or the fact that I was going to smell like charred food and wet jeans when I went to go meet this wedding planner.

"You're going to need to hire a new cook," Everett whispered.

I looked at my brother, at the man who did his best to make sure we didn't go bankrupt, and I wanted to just grumble. "I figured."

"I can help for now, but you know I'm only part-time. I can't stay away from my twins for too long," Sandy said as she came forward to take the pan off the stove. "I wish I could do full time, but this is all I can do for now."

Sandy had come back from maternity leave after we had already opened the retreat. She had been on with the former owners and was brilliant. But she had a right to be a mom and not want to work full time. I understood that, and I knew that Sandy didn't want to handle a whole kitchen by herself. She liked her position as a sous chef.

I was going to have to figure out what to do. Again.

"I'll get it done," I said while rubbing my temples.

"You know what we need to do," Everett whispered, and I shook my head.

"He'll kill us."

"Maybe, but it'll be worth it in the end. And speaking of, don't you have that interview soon? Or do you want me to take it?" His gaze tracked to my jeans.

I shook my head. "No, help Sandy."

Everett winced. "Just because I know how to slice an onion, it doesn't mean I'm good at cooking."

"I'm sorry, did you just say you could slice an onion? Get to it," Sandy put in with a smile, pointing at the sink. "Wash those hands."

"I cannot believe I just said that out loud. I just stepped right into it," Everett said with a sigh. "Go to the interview. You know what to ask."

"I do. And I hope we don't get screwed this time."

"You know, if we're lucky, we'll get someone as good as Roy's wedding planner, or at least that woman that we met. You know who she is." Everett grinned like a cat with the canary.

I narrowed my eyes. "Don't bring her up."

"Oh, I can't help it. A single dance, and you were drawn to her."

"What dance? You know what? No, I don't have time. We have to work on lunch and dinner. Tell me while you work," Sandy added with a wink.

Everett leaned toward her as he washed his hands.

"Well, you see, there was this dance, and he met the perfect woman, and then she got engaged."

Sandy's eyes widened. "Engaged? How did that happen? She was dating someone else?" she asked as she looked at me.

I pinched the bridge of my nose. "It was at Roy's place when we were looking at the venue to see if we wanted to buy the retreat here." I sighed, I knew if I just let it all out, she would move on from this conversation, and I would never have to deal with it again. "Somehow, I ended up at a wedding there, caught the garter. This woman caught the bouquet, and she happened to be the wedding planner. We danced, we laughed, and as she walked away, her boyfriend got down on one knee and proposed."

"No way!" She leaned forward with a fierce look on her face, her eyes bright. "What did she say?"

"I have no clue. I left." I ignored whatever feeling might want to show up at that thought. Everett gave me a glance, and I shook my head. "Enough of that. Yes, the wedding that she did was great, but I honestly have no idea who she is, and she has a job. She doesn't need to work here." And I didn't know what I would do if I saw her again or had to work with her. There had been such an intense connection that I knew it would be awkward as hell. But thankfully, she had her own business and wasn't going to come to the Wilder Retreat for a job.

I left Sandy and Everett on their own, knowing that they were capable, at least for now. And I knew who we would have to hire if she said yes, and if my other brother didn't kill me first.

I washed my hands in the sink on the way out, grateful that at least I looked somewhat decent, if not a little disheveled, and made my way out front, hoping that the wedding planner who came in through the doors would be the one that would stick. Because we needed some good luck. After the day we've had, we needed some good luck.

I turned the corner and nearly tripped over my feet.

Because, of course, fate was this way.

It was her.

Of all the wedding planners from all the wedding venues, it was her.

In the mood to read another family saga? Meet the Wilder Brothers in One Way Back to Me!

From Bittersweet Promises

Leif

"Not only did you convince me to somehow go on a blind date, it became a double date. How on earth did you work this magic on me, cousin?" I asked Lake as she leaned against the pillar just inside the restaurant.

Lake grinned at me, her dark hair pulled away from her face. She had on this swingy black dress and looked as if she were excited, anxious, nervous, and happy all at the same time. Considering she was bouncing on her toes when usually Lake was calm, cool, and collected, was saying something. "I asked, and you said yes. Because you love me."

"I might love you because we're family, but I still think we're making a mistake." I shook my head and pulled at my shirt sleeves. Lake had somehow convinced me to wear a button-up shirt tucked into gray pants, I even had on shiny shoes. I looked like a damn banker. But if that's what Lake wanted, that's what I would do.

Lake might technically be my cousin, even though we weren't blood-related, but we were more like brother and sister than any of my other cousins.

I had siblings, as did Lake, but with the generational gap, we were at least a decade older than all of our other cousins. That meant, despite the fact that we had lived over an hour apart for most of our lives, we'd grown up more like siblings.

I loved my three younger siblings and talked to them daily. Unlike some blended families, they *were* my brothers and sister and not like strangers or distant family members. I didn't feel a disconnect from the three of them, but Lake was still closer to me.

Probably because we were either heading into our thirties or already there, where most of our other cousins were either just now in their early twenties or still teenagers in high school. With how big we Montgomerys were as a family, it made sense that there would be such a widespread age group. That meant that Lake and I were best friends, cousins, practically siblings, and sometimes the banes of each other's existences.

We were also business owners and partners and saw each other too often these days. That was probably why she convinced me to go on a blind double date. But she had been out with Zach before. I, however, had never met May. Lake had some connection with her that I wasn't sure about, and for some reason Lake's date had said yes to this double date.

And, in the complicated way of family, I had agreed to it. I must have been tired. Or perhaps I'd had too many beers. Because I didn't do blind dates, and recently, I didn't do dates at all.

Lake scanned her phone, then looked up at me, all innocence in her smart gaze. "You shouldn't have told me you wanted to settle down in your old age."

I narrowed my eyes. "I'm still in my early thirties, jerk. Stop calling me old."

"I shouldn't call you old since you're only a few years older than me." She fluttered her eyelashes and I flipped her off, ignoring the stare from the older woman next to me. Though I was a tattoo artist, I didn't have many visible tattoos. Most of mine were on my back and legs, hidden from the world unless I wanted to show them. I hadn't figured out what I wanted on my arms beyond a few small pieces on my wrists and upper shoulders. And since tattoos were permanent, I was taking my time. If a client needed to see my skin with ink to feel comfortable, I'd show them my back. My body was a canvas, so I did what I could to set people at ease.

But I still had the eyebrow piercing and had recently taken out my nose ring. I didn't look too scary for most people. But apparently, flipping off a woman, growling, and cursing a time or two in front of strangers probably made me appear too close to the dark side.

"Yes, I want to settle down, but this will be awkward, won't it? Where the two of us are strangers, and the two of you aren't?" I wanted a life, a future, and yeah, one day to settle down with someone. I just didn't know why I'd mentioned it to Lake in the first place.

"If it helps, May doesn't know Zach, either. So it's a group of strangers, except I know everybody." She clapped her hands together and did her version of an evil laugh, and I just shook my head.

"Considering what you do for a living and how you like to manipulate things in your way, this makes sense. Are you going to be adding a matchmaking company to your conglomerate?"

Lake just fluttered her eyelashes again and laughed. Lake owned a small tech company that made a shit ton of money over the past couple of years. And because she was brilliant at what she did, innovative, and liked pushing money towards women-owned businesses, she owned more than one company at this point and was an investor in mine. I wouldn't be surprised if she found a way to open up a women-owned matchmaking company right here in town.

"It might be fun. I can call it Montgomery Links." Her eyes went wide. "Oh, my God. I have to write that down." She pulled out her phone, began to take notes, and I pinched the bridge of my nose.

"You know I trust you with my actual life, but I don't know if I trust you with my dating life."

Lake tossed her hair behind her shoulder as she continued to type. "Shut up. You love me. And once I finish setting you up, the rest of the family's next."

"Oh, really? You're going to get Daisy and Noah next?" I asked, speaking of two more of our cousins.

"Maybe. Of course, Sebastian's the only one of the younger group that seems to have a serious girlfriend."

I nodded, speaking of our other familial business partner. Sebastian was still a teenager, though in college. He had wanted to open up Montgomery Ink Legacy with me, the full title of our company. There was a legacy to it, and Sebastian had wanted in. So, though he didn't work there full-time, he was putting his future towards us. And in the ways of young love, he and his girlfriend had been together since middle school. The fact that my younger cousin was better at relationships than I was didn't make me feel great. But I was going to ignore that.

"You're not going to start up a matchmaking service, are you? Or maybe an app?"

"Dating apps are ridiculous these days, they practically want you to invest in coins to bid on dates, and that's not something I'm in the mood for. But maybe there's something I can try. I'll add it to my list."

Lake's list of inventions and tech was notorious, and knowing the brilliance of my cousin, she would one day rule the world and might eventually cross everything off that list.

"Oh, here's Zach." Lake's face brightened immediately, and she smiled up at a man with dark hair, piercing gray eyes, and an actual dimple on his cheek.

Tonight was not only about my blind date, but me getting the lay of the land when it came to Zach. I was the first step into meeting the family. Oh, if Zach passed my gauntlet, he would meet the rest of the Montgomerys, and we were mighty. All one hundred of us.

"Zach, you're here." Lake's voice went soft, and she went on her tiptoes even in her high heels as Zach pressed a soft kiss to her lips.

"Of course, I'm here. And you're early, as usual."

Lake blushed and ducked her head. "Well, you know me. I like to be early because being on time is late," she said at the same time I did, mumbling under my breath. It was a familiar refrain when it came to us.

"Zach, good to meet you," I said, holding out my hand.

The other man gripped it firmly and shook. "Nice to meet you too, Leif. I know you might be the one on a blind date soon, but I'm nervous."

I chuckled, shaking my head. "Yeah, I'm pretty nervous too. Though I'm grateful that Lake's trying to look out for me."

My cousin laughed softly. "You totally were not saying that a few minutes ago, but be suave and sophisticated now. Or just be yourself, May's on her way."

I met Zach's gaze and we both rolled our eyes. When I turned toward the door, I saw a woman of average height, with black straight hair, green eyes, and a sweet smile. I didn't know much about May, other than Lake knew her and liked her. If I was going to start dating again after taking time off to get the rest of my life together, I might as well start with someone that one of my best friends liked.

"May, I'm so glad that you're here," Lake said as she hugged the other woman tightly.

As Lake began to bounce on her heels, I realized

that my cousin's cool, calm, and collected exterior was only for work. She was bouncing and happy when it came to her friends or when she was nervous. I knew that, of course, but I had forgotten how she had turned into the mogul that she was. It was good to see her relaxed and happy.

Now I just needed to figure out how to do that for myself.

May stood in front of me, and I felt like I was starting middle school all over again. A new school, a new life, and a past that didn't make much sense to anyone else.

I swallowed hard and nodded, not putting out my hand to shake, thinking that would be weird, but I also didn't want to hug her. I didn't even know this woman. Why was everything so awkward? Instead, I lifted my chin. "Hello, May. It's nice to meet you. Lake says only good things."

There, smooth. Not really. Zach began to move out of frame, with Lake at his side as the two went to speak to the hostess, leaving May and me alone.

This wasn't going to be awkward at all.

The woman just smiled at me, her eyes wide. "It's nice to meet you, too. And Lake does speak highly of you. Also, this is very awkward, so I'm so sorry if I say something stupid. I know that your cousin said that I should be set up with you which is great but I'm not great at blind dates and apparently this is a double date and now I'm going to stop talking." She said the words so quickly they all ran into one breath.

I shook my head and laughed. "We're on the same page there."

"Okay, good. It's nice to meet you, Leif Montgomery."

"And it's nice to meet you too, May."

We made our way to Lake and Zach, who had gotten our table, and we all sat down, talking about work and other things. May was in child life development, taught online classes, and was also a nanny.

"I'm actually about to start with a new family soon. I'm excited. I know that being a nanny isn't something that most people strive for, or at least that's what they tell you, but I love being able to work with children and be the person that is there when a single parent or even both parents are out in the workforce, trying to do everything."

I nodded, taking a sip of my beer. "I get you completely. With how my parents worked, I was lucky that they were able to get childcare within the buildings. Since they each owned their own businesses, they made it work. But my family worked long hours, and that's why I ended up being the babysitter a lot of the times when childcare wasn't an option." I cleared my throat. "I'm a lot older than a lot of my cousins," I added.

"Both of us are, but I'm glad that you only said yourself," Lake said, grinning. She leaned into Zach as she spoke, the four of us in a horseshoe-shaped booth. That gave May and me space since this was a first date and still awkward as hell, and so Lake and Zach could cuddle. Not that that was something I needed to be a part of.

"Oh, I'm glad that you didn't judge. The last few dates that I've been on they always gave me weird looks because I think they expected a nanny to be this old crone or someone that's looking for a different job." She shrugged and continued. "When I eventually get married and maybe even start a family, I want to continue my job. I like being there to help another family achieve their goals. And I can't believe I just said start a family on my first date. And that I mentioned that I've been on a few other dates." She let out a breath. "I'm notoriously bad at dating. Like, the worst. Just warning you."

I laughed, shaking my head. "I'm rusty at it, so don't worry." And even though I said that, I had a feeling that May felt no spark towards me, and I didn't feel anything towards her. She was nice and pleasant, and I could probably consider her a friend one day. But there wasn't any spark. May's eyes weren't dancing. She wasn't leaning forward, trying to touch my hand across the table. We were just sitting there casually, enjoying a really good steak, as Lake and Zach enjoyed their date.

By the end of dinner, I didn't want dessert, and neither did May, so we said goodbye to the other couple, who decided to stay. I walked May to her car, ignoring Lake's warning look, but I didn't know what exactly she was warning me about.

"Thanks for dinner," May said. "I could have paid. I know this is a blind date and all that, but you didn't have to pay."

I shook my head. "I paid for the four of us because I wanted to be nice. I'll make Lake pay next time."

May beamed. "Yes, I like that. You guys are a good family."

"Anyway," I said, clearing my throat as I stuck my hands in my pockets. "I guess I'll see you around."

May just looked at me, threw her head back, and laughed. "You're right. You are rusty at this."

"Sorry." Heat flushed my skin, and I resisted the urge to tug on my eyebrow ring.

"It's okay. No spark. I'm used to it. I don't spark well."

"May, I'm sorry." I cringed. "It's not you."

"Oh, God, please don't say that. 'It's not you. It's me.

You're working on yourself. You're just so busy with work.' I've heard it all."

"Seriously?" I asked. May was hot. Nice, but there just wasn't a spark.

She shrugged. "It's okay. I'll probably see you around sometime because I am friends with Lake. However, I am perfectly fine having this be our one and only. You'll find your person. It's okay that it's not me." And with that, she got in the car and left, leaving me standing there.

Well then. Tonight wasn't horrible, but it wasn't great. I got in my car, and instead of heading home where I'd be alone, watching something on some streaming service while I drank a beer and pretended that I knew what I was doing with my life, I headed into Montgomery Ink Legacy.

We were the third branch of the company and the first owned by our generation. Montgomery Ink was the tattoo shop in downtown Denver. While there were open spots for some walk-ins and special circumstances, my father, aunt, and their team had years' worth of waiting lists. They worked their asses off and made sure to get in everybody that they could, but people wanted Austin Montgomery's art. Same with my aunt, Maya.

There was another tattoo shop down in Colorado Springs, owned by my parents' cousins, who I just called aunt and uncle because we were close enough that using real titles for everybody got confusing. Montgomery Ink Too was thriving down there, and they had waiting lists as well. My family could have opened more shops and gone nationwide, even global if they wanted to, but they liked keeping it how it was, in the family and those connected.

We were a branch, but our own in the making. I had gone into business with Lake, of course, and Sebastian, when he was ready, as well as Nick. Nick was my best friend. I had known him for ages, and he had wanted to be part of something as well. He might not be a Montgomery by name, but he had eaten over at my family's house enough times throughout the years that he was practically a Montgomery. And he had invested in the company as well, and so now we were nearly a year into owning the shop and trying not to fail.

I pulled into the parking lot, grateful it was still open since we didn't close until nine most nights, and greeted Nick, who was still working.

Sebastian was in the back, going over sketches with a client, and I nodded at him. He might be eighteen, but he was still in training, an apprentice, and was working his ass off to learn.

"Date sucked then?" Sebastian asked, and Nick just rolled his eyes and went back to work on a client's wrist.

"I don't want to talk about it," I groaned.

The rest of the staff was off since Nick would close up on his own. Sebastian was just there since he didn't have homework or a date with Marley.

"Was she hot at least?" Sebastian asked, and the client, a woman in her sixties, bopped him on the head with her bag gently.

"Sebastian Montgomery. Be nice."

Sebastian blushed. "Sorry, Mrs. Anderson."

I looked over at the woman and grinned. "Hi, Mrs. Anderson. It's nice to see you out of the classroom."

She narrowed her eyes at me, even though they filled with laughter. "I needed my next Jane Austen tattoo, thank you very much," the older woman said as she went back to working with Sebastian. She had been my and then Sebastian's English teacher. The fact that she was on her fifth tattoo with some literary quote told me that I had been damn lucky in most of my teachers growing up.

She was kick-ass, and I had a feeling that she would let Sebastian do the tattoo for her rather than just have him work on the design with me as we did for most of the people who came in. He had learned under my father and was working under me now. It was strange to think that he wasn't a little kid anymore. But he was in a long-term relationship, kicking ass in college, and knew what he wanted to do with his life.

I might know what I want to do with my work life, but everything else seemed a little off.

"So it didn't work out?" Nick asked as he walked up to the front desk with the clients after going over aftercare.

"Not really," I said, looking down at my phone.

The client, a woman in her mid-twenties with bright pink hair, a lip ring, and kind eyes, leaned over the desk to look at me.

"You'll find someone, Leif. Don't worry."

I looked at our regular and shook my head. "Thanks, Kim. Too bad that you don't swing this way."

I winked as I said it, a familiar refrain from both of us.

Kim was married to a woman named Sonya, and the two of them were happy and working on in vitro with donated sperm for their first kid.

"Hey, I'm sorry too that I'm a lesbian. I'll never know what it means to have Leif Montgomery. Or any Montgomery, since I found my love far too quickly. I mean, what am I ever going to do not knowing the love of a Montgomery?"

Mrs. Anderson chuckled from her chair, Sebastian

held back a snort, and I just looked at Nick, who rolled his eyes and helped Kim out of the place.

I was tired, but it was okay. The date wasn't all bad. May was nice. But it felt like I didn't have much right then.

And then Nick sat in front of me, scowled, and I realized that I did have something. I had my friends and my family. I didn't need much more.

"So, you and May didn't work out?"

I raised a brow. "You knew her name? Did I tell you that?"

Nick shook his head. "Lake did."

That made sense, considering the two of them spoke as much as we did. "So, was it your idea to set me up on a blind date?"

"Fuck no. That was all Lake. I just do what she says. Like we all do."

I sighed and went through my appointments for the next day. "We're busy for the next month. That's good, right?" I asked.

"You're the business genius here. I just play with ink. But yes, that's good. Now, don't let your cousin set you up any more dates. Find them for yourself. You know what you're doing."

"So says the man who dates less than me."

"That's what you think. I'm more private about it.

As it should be." I flipped him off as he stood up, then he gestured towards a stack of bills in the corner. "You have a few personal things that made their way here. Don't want you to miss out on them before you head home."

"Thanks, bro."

"No problem. I'm going to help Sebastian with his consult, and then I'll clean up. You should head home. Though you're doing it alone, so I feel sorry for you."

"Fuck you," I called out.

"Fuck you, too."

"Boys," Mrs. Anderson said, in that familiar English teacher refrain, and both Nick and I cringed before saying, "Sorry," simultaneously.

Sebastian snickered, then went back to work, and I headed towards the edge of the counter, picking up the stack of papers. Most were bills, some were random papers that needed to be filed or looked over. Some were just junk mail. But there was one letter, written in block print that didn't look familiar. Chills went up my spine and I opened it, wondering what the fuck this was. Maybe it was someone asking to buy my house. I got a lot of handwritten letters for that, but I didn't think this was going to be that. I swallowed hard, slid open the paper, and froze.

"I'll find you, boy. Oops. Looks like I already did. Be waiting. I know you miss me."

I let the paper hit the top of the counter and swallowed hard, trying to remain cool so I didn't worry anyone else.

I didn't know exactly who that was from, but I had a horrible feeling that they wouldn't wait long to tell me.

Read the rest in Bittersweet Promises!
OUT NOW!

About the Author

Carrie Ann Ryan is the New York Times and USA Today bestselling author of contemporary, paranormal, and young adult romance. Her works include the Montgomery Ink, Redwood Pack, Fractured Connections, and Elements of Five series, which have sold over 3.0 million books worldwide. She started writing while in graduate school for her advanced degree in chemistry and hasn't stopped since. Carrie Ann has written over seventy-five novels and novellas with more in the works. When she's not losing herself in her emotional and action-packed worlds, she's reading as much as she can while wrangling her clowder of cats who have more followers than she does.

www.CarrieAnnRyan.com

www.ingramcontent.com/pod-product-compliance
Lightning Source LLC
Chambersburg PA
CBHW011144100726
47899CB00010B/3158